EMBELLISH

EMBELLISH

Kelley Connor

ABSOLUTELY AMAZING eBOOKS

ABSOLUTELY AMAZING eBOOKS

Published by Whiz Bang LLC, 926 Truman Avenue, Key West, Florida 33040, USA.

For information contact:
Publisher@AbsolutelyAmazingEbooks.com

ISBN-13: 978-1945772788 (Absolutely Amazing Ebooks)
ISBN-10: 1945772786

To my M&Ms whose faith and love keep me going.

To J. who continues to support me no matter what line I am walking.

EMBELLISH

PROLOGUE

Jennifer Fall helplessly watched Cory, her eight-year-old daughter, lying in the hospital bed. She looked so pale and tiny; her fragility emphasized by the sheer number of medical devices attached to her body, keeping her alive.

Over the last several weeks, Jennifer had become a fixture at the hospital. She was no longer rattled by the beeping, pinging, dripping, or humming noises surrounding her. The strong smell of disinfectant and sickness no longer stung her nose as she sat waiting in the hard, straight-backed orange chair with metal armrests. She sat nearly motionless hour after hour. The only thing she could think about was her daughter waking up. The doctors had all warned her that Cory might not be the same, and that was if she woke up at all. Despite all their tests, they couldn't tell how her brain might have been affected by the trauma, blood loss, and smoke inhalation.

Jennifer tried not to spend time thinking about the future and what it might hold. She could only focus on getting through one hour at a time. The waiting felt endless. It was like her life had been paused in her own personal living hell. At least now, she tried to console herself, Cory was breathing on her own. It was a lot better than she was doing a few days ago. It had to mean something, even if the doctors didn't want her to become too optimistic.

Jennifer rubbed her eyes. They felt permanently swollen from the tears that were always so close to the surface. She was bone tired and emotionally drained. She had to fight to keep her eyes open. She couldn't risk closing them; she was too afraid she would fall asleep.

When she slept all her fears and anxiety played out in her nightmares.

Her anxiety stemmed from three main issues. The first was the trauma her daughter went through. No child should have to go through what Cory did. No mother, for that matter, should have to witness it. The second was the fear that Cory would never regain consciousness and she'd never see her beautiful smile again. The last problem was the panic she felt over the possibility that Cory would live and that she had the family gift.

Although, family curse might be a better description, she thought with disdain. It made her blood run cold to think what having the gift could mean for her. Jennifer blinked a few times before focusing on her daughter's angelic heart-shaped face. She couldn't risk anything happening to her daughter again. She wasn't sure she'd be able to live through it.

Right now, her family assumed she finally found her own gift. They assumed her words had been enough to keep Cory alive. They did think it was unusual for the gift to surface so late in life and for it to be strong enough to prevent death. However, in this case, it seemed so clearly expressed. Nobody had any doubt that Cory was alive because of her.

That night was painfully burned into Jennifer's mind. Her sister, Miranda, had driven her to her ex-husband's house when they found out what he had done. They had to park blocks away because of all the emergency vehicles on the scene. They ran toward the house but were stopped by a police officer. Jennifer tried to explain to the officer who she was, but the only sounds she could make were sobs, screams, and dry heaves. She desperately needed Cory. She had to get to her, but the officer kept her from running. He held her tightly, pinning her arms to her sides, effectively keeping her from the chaos of the burning house.

"I'm so sorry." He said over and over as she wailed while her sister, Miranda, watched in horror. "The little girl didn't make it." He finally whispered.

Jennifer remembered every single detail about that night. She remembered how she fell to her knees when she heard those words leave his mouth.

"No." She had cried. "No, she didn't die. She is alive. She didn't die. I need to get to her."

She wailed in anguish as her sister's arms replaced the officer's. Jennifer didn't know how much time passed before her gut-wrenching sobs slowed.

"Ma'am," a man dressed as a paramedic got her attention by gently touching her shoulder. The police officer was nowhere to be seen. "I thought you would like to know, the ambulance has just left. They've gone to United Children's. Perhaps someone could drive you so you can be there when they work on her."

Jennifer tried to make her mouth form the question, but it seemed to be incapable of speech. She heard Miranda's voice crying the words she wanted to get out. "What? What are you talking about?"

The man looked nervous. "I thought," he stammered looking from Miranda to Jennifer, "I thought you were the family."

"We are. I am." Jennifer finally managed through the snot, sobs, and tears. "I am her mother. What are you saying?"

"Just that the ambulance just left. We thought we lost her, the team did everything they could. They didn't think it was enough. They stopped resuscitation measures. But then, as they were cleaning up, they heard her groan and realized...." His voice drifted off before he continued, "they realized she was still alive." He paused to shake his head in awe.

Stunned, Jennifer watched as the paramedic took

a deep breath and squared his shoulders before he continued. "We were able to get her stabilized here on the ground. I have to warn you, it doesn't look good. Chances are not good, but they just left for United Children's. I thought you would want to know so you could get there." His eyes burned with sincere compassion.

Jennifer remembered the ragged breath she dragged into her lungs as her eyes met her sister's eyes. She wanted to leave immediately to get to the hospital. She felt overwhelming relief that her daughter might still be alive. Cory might somehow pull through. Miranda's eyes did not reflect relief, they were filled with panic.

In her head, Jennifer knew Miranda was right to be worried. Because of their family gift, everyone understood they were not to influence life or death. It simply wasn't done, but then the gift had never been manifested in either Jennifer or Miranda before. They knew the rules. Everyone in the family knew the rules, but since they didn't have the gift, they had never thought about them as anything other than abstract concepts. Plus, there had to be at least an element of truth for words to become reality. Cory was supposedly already dead. Jennifer had never meant to change fate when she cried that the officer was wrong and Cory was alive. In her heart, she was simply a mother who refused to lose her world.

Jennifer knew she would be watched now that the family thought she was gifted. She would never admit to anyone, not even Miranda, that it wasn't her that had changed everything. She also knew it wasn't Miranda because she hadn't uttered a word. Nobody, except Jennifer, suspected it could have been Cory herself who had the gift. Everyone else believed Cory was too injured and far too young to have it, but who else could it have been?

Logically Jennifer knew Cory was too young. But it had to have been her. Nobody else from the family had been there that night and Jennifer tested herself ten days after the incident.

Her test happened late one night. The hospital was unusually quiet and Jennifer's favorite nurse, Bailey Hutchinson, was on duty. Jennifer sucked in a deep breath and had her test.

"Bailey," Jennifer intentionally lied, "Cory is doing so well. She woke up a little while ago and nothing was wrong with her. She had no problems coming out of her coma. She's made a full recovery." Jennifer's teal colored eyes stared earnestly at Bailey's shocked expression. If she had the gift, Cory would be awake and doing well. If she didn't, Bailey might think she was crazy.

Jennifer watched Bailey look over Cory's broken, unmoving form. She could tell that Bailey thought the stress had finally made her snap. Bailey said nothing as she left the room. She returned a short time later with a warm blanket and an extra pillow. Silently, the nurse pushed her chair into its reclining position and tucked her in as if she was a small child. Bailey gave her a small sad smile and told her she had to get a good night sleep.

Jennifer wasn't surprised her words didn't change Cory's condition. She didn't think she had the gift and her test confirmed it.

Jennifer tried to reassure herself that it hadn't been the gift that saved her daughter. She wanted to believe it might have happened the way the paramedic said. Maybe they had made a mistake when they told her she was dead, then they heard her and they got her help. Maybe nobody interfered with anything and she was worried for no reason.

She wished her speculation that they had made a

mistake was true, but in her heart, she knew it wasn't.

Jennifer didn't want to think about what the risks would be for Cory if she held a powerful version of the gift. According to the family legends, if she had a powerful gift she would be hunted, enticed to create false truths, have her powers stolen, or killed to obstruct her interference.

Jennifer couldn't let anything happen to Cory, especially now that she had come so close to losing her already. She would make sure Coy was always protected no matter what. She would have to let the family see her, but she would keep them at a distance. She didn't want them to get too close. She would continue to let them think that she had the power and that she followed the rules perfectly. She would never let them suspect anything else. They would have no need to intervene.

Her only purpose was to make sure Cory was safe. Now more than ever.

CHAPTER 1
8 years later

She stood in her towel looking into the spot she wiped clear in her steamy bathroom mirror. Her skin was so pale it was almost translucent. Of course, her coloring was naturally pale, but it was emphasized because her skin was always hidden under so much makeup it was never touched by the sun. She held her towel open to study her body in the reflection. Her body was tall and slender, not muscular, but delicate. Unfortunately, it was enviable.

The corners of her doll-like mouth twisted into a frown. She wished she looked different. Her eyes were beautifully round and a startling shade of teal blue. Her small nose was straight with a slight upturn. Her cheekbones were high and her neck long, giving her the look of a graceful dancer, even in her stillness.

The last thing Cory Fall ever wanted to do was draw attention to herself. It bothered her that she was beautiful. She did what she could to hide it and keep others away.

Her long hair hung in a single solid mass down her back. She rarely brushed it. She kept it limp and tangled. She leaned in toward the mirror, studying the pale blond roots visible under her flat black dye job. She would have to leave a note for her mom to let her know she needed more black dye.

Since she didn't know how long it would be until she could get the dye, she walked into her room and rummaged through her overstuffed desk crammed with mostly filled notebooks, nearly empty tubes of paint, and overused brushes. Finally, she pulled out the black sharpie marker she had been hunting for.

She studied her reflection in her dresser mirror, leaned forward so her face was almost touching the glass, and colored in all the blond roots she could see. She didn't care that she sometimes discolored her skin. It would add to her look.

The look that told everyone else to stay away.

She rummaged through her drawers and pulled out several layers of heavy, shapeless, black clothes splattered haphazardly with dots of colored paint stains.

She slipped her feet into a pair of ugly black clogs and walked back into the bathroom to start her makeup.

She pulled out her makeup bag and rummaged in it finally finding her tweezers. She stood on her tip toes and leaned in toward the bathroom mirror, searching for any stray eyebrow hairs that dared to grow. She used to dye her light brown eyebrows black like her hair, but she noticed the black eyebrows drew attention to her eyes so she plucked them out, every last hair. She didn't try to draw them back in. Her face looked somehow flawed, unbalanced without eyebrows. She preferred it that way.

She coated her face with a thick layer of pale foundation. She liked the way it evened her skin, making it flat and bland. Sometimes she colored her lips deep burgundy or black, but today she rubbed her foundation coated fingertips across her lips. It canceled out their natural pink color and made them a sickly chalky peach that blended her face into a flat plain.

She was good at disguising her looks. She needed people to look past her. She wanted to blend into the background. She didn't want to be acknowledged, she felt safer being ignored. Her biggest problem was disguising her eyes. They were wide and innocent with a color common in her estranged family photos, but unique in the world. People couldn't help but notice them.

She hid her eyes the best she could by encircling them unflatteringly with black kohl liner in a thick dark circle. She forced people to notice her striking, off-putting makeup rather than her beautiful features.

Finally, she pulled her hair back into a messy bun and gathered her tattered black backpack. She didn't have books or a purse. She didn't need them at her special school.

Her school didn't offer much in the way of academics. She knew how to read and balance a checkbook, they taught her that much. But at her school, there wasn't much expected of students. Her school was a place where kids with physical or emotional problems could go and not get into trouble during the day. Teaching them anything was a bonus.

Every once in a while, the school counselor would pull her out of class and talk about her future. He probably did it to meet some funding guidelines set up by the state. She didn't care about her future and she didn't think he did either. She knew she was only eligible to stay at the school until she was twenty-one years old, five years away. At her school, they held graduation ceremonies whenever a kid had their twenty-first birthday. It was a big deal. The kid would wear a graduation cap and gown all day as they attended classes. People would congratulate them and shake their hand. Then, at some point during the day, they would take a group picture and everyone would celebrate with a piece of cake. The next day the kid would be gone. They would never be seen at the school again.

Cory couldn't imagine her life in five years and tried not to think about what she would do after she left the school. She never answered the counselor's questions. She just stared at him, slightly awed that he continued to ask her what she thought. She knew from her sessions with the counselor that she would probably move into a group home when she aged out of the school. Her counselor tried to make the group home sound like a good thing. She knew there would be six to ten residents of the home with a live-in caregiver to oversee their lives.

Cory tried to care, but she couldn't. She knew she would spend her days painting at the group home much like she spent her days painting at her school now. She didn't think it mattered where she was when she painted. So, it didn't matter if she ended up in a group home.

She loved to draw and paint. She spent most of her time at home and at school doing it. Although she used oil and acrylic paints, watercolors were her favorite. She loved setting up the paper on the easel, using water to prep, and then touching the color to the wet paper and watching it seep outward as if it had a life of its own. Of course, she also used pastels, pencils, charcoal, really whatever she had available. When she was doing art, she didn't think about anything else, and that was a good thing.

She made her way to the kitchen, poured herself some orange juice, and waited for her mother to take her to school.

Five minutes later, her mother was ready to go. She chattered at Cory while she made a piece of peanut butter toast for breakfast, telling her what the plan was for the day. She even asked Cory questions about what she would be doing at school that day. They both knew full well Cory would never answer her questions.

Cory hadn't spoken since she was 8 years old. She wasn't even sure she still could. She had no desire to try. She felt like her tongue was glued to the roof of her mouth, a useless glob of an appendage.

She saw her mother glance at the picture of her in the living room. It was from a photoshoot they had done for a series of commercials when she was about seven and a half years old, right before everything happened. In the picture, Cory was small and blond. Her big, bright, curious eyes were her most prominent feature. Her smile was impishly happy, while the gap in between her front teeth added to her approachable beauty rather than detracting from it.

Cory knew it was a photo of her, but she couldn't remember having been that girl. She couldn't remember much of anything from before. It was like there was one life before, a life that didn't belong to her, then it happened, and then there was after. She lived in the after and that was all there was.

CHAPTER 2

Cory was thrilled to be the first to enter the art room. The shabby room had been painted bright white several years ago. The furniture consisted of older metal stools, a few large tables, and several easels of different sizes. The room should have felt institutionalized and dingy, but it didn't, at least not to her. The wall opposite the door was made up of grime-covered oversized windows that let in the perfect amount of light. At least perfect for painting. To her, this room felt like home.

Cory was pretty sure if she ever decided to talk again, it would be in this room. She felt a lightness when she was in the room like she could talk if she had something she wanted to say out loud. Between the room and her art, she could escape. Being in the class and getting lost in her paintings made her feel like she was existing in a place where she didn't worry, hurt, or feel self-consciousness. It was blissful.

There weren't many kids at the school who took art classes, and certainly not to the extent Cory did. Many of the student schedules were packed with courses on what the school termed "activities of daily living." Since Cory already knew how to dress herself and make a sandwich, she didn't have to go to them. She was allowed to work on her art alone in the classroom with the condition teachers and staff would randomly check on her and she would lose the privilege if she was ever doing anything she shouldn't be.

She did, however, have to suffer through the "fundamentals of household management" and "on the job expectations" courses offered at the school, but she mostly daydreamed her way through the sessions.

The thing with not talking was that people assumed she was incapable or most likely, stupid. She wasn't. She just didn't talk and rarely completed tests or worksheets put in front of her. She didn't see the point.

Her counselors and teachers over the years didn't know what to do with her. They tried different ways of getting her to interact, but they quickly gave up in defeat. Her own mother didn't know what to do with her. The only thing anyone could do was enroll her in her special school and hope for the best.

She was okay with it. She didn't want to go to a regular school. She wanted to be ignored and allowed to paint. Her life, such that it was, worked for her.

She set up her easel and started sketching out a scene in pencil with a light hand. She wanted to explore light and dark in an abstract landscape. She closed her eyes and imagined, then she let her pencil glide softly over the paper.

As she finished blocking out her sketch, the door to the classroom banged open and a loud cry echoed through the room.

The classroom aid was bringing Jess and Thomas into the room for their art period. She didn't know which of them had cried out or why they did it. They didn't do much. They were both in special wheelchairs that seemed to encase their bodies like a cage. Neither one could purposely move. Like her, neither one spoke.

Cory had overheard teachers talking one time and knew Thomas was the victim of a near-drowning when he was five. He had lived, but when his eyes were open, they were fixed upward toward the ceiling. Cory often wondered how aware he was of his surroundings. She thought she should feel sorry for him, but she didn't really. Maybe it was good to be him. Maybe he was living a different reality in his mind where he could just be and nobody would ever expect anything of him. She didn't like to feel even a twinge of jealousy over Thomas's situation, but she did. She couldn't help it.

Jess, on the other hand, was aware. She couldn't move her body because of a rare neuromuscular condition she had been born with. Nobody told Cory Jess was aware, but she could see it in the girl's eyes. Jess's hazel eyes knew what was going on. They were intelligent. She saw her surroundings, she saw things and people, but she could never respond with anything other than an occasional blink or moan. Her face was frozen into an expressionless mask with an open mouth. Her classroom aid constantly put ChapStick on her lips because they became so dry. Cory felt connected to Jess, like she knew her and maybe they were friends. She understood Jess's moods by looking into her eyes. She knew Jess had good days and bad days just like everyone else. She could tell when Jess liked what was going on and when she didn't. Cory hated that other people didn't seem to know how to read her the way she did. Most people weren't observant enough to know what was going on with anyone other than themselves.

Cory knew Jess liked being in the art room. She hoped Thomas liked being there too, wherever his mind was. Sometimes the aid would park them facing the window. Sometimes they faced her. Other times, the aid would hold a paintbrush dipped in color in their hands and move it across a piece of paper for them, like they were painting.

Today, the aid, Cory thought her name was Melissa, looked uncomfortable.

"Umm, Cory," she started, "I really need to use the restroom. I know I am not supposed to, but do you think you could keep an eye on Jess and Thomas for just a minute?"

Cory stared at her. She had never been responsible for anyone else before, ever. She wondered if she could do it, but didn't know why she wouldn't be able to. It wasn't like they were going to go anywhere and nobody expected her to do anything except paint. She shrugged her shoulders in a way that led Melissa to believe she was okay to be left for a moment.

"Thanks, Cory. I will be back in a minute." Melissa said as she hustled out of the room.

Cory turned toward her easel, ready to get started, but then paused. She was responsible for someone besides herself. She pivoted to look over at Jess and Thomas.

As usual, their bodies were contorted in frozen positions. Jess had a blue blanket tucked across her lap while Thomas had a gray blanket wrapped around his legs. Thomas stared at the ceiling, with no light of comprehension. Jess's eyes looked lost.

Cory wondered if she was confused at being left alone. Or maybe she was having a difficult time today. She could be angry about something.

Cory tilted her head and studied Jess for a moment. She wanted to talk to her and tell her things would be okay, but her own limp tongue was unable to form the words. She swallowed and turned back to her workstation.

She hesitated and then pulled a new sea sponge from her drawer. She picked up her clean glass of water, the water she had gotten ready to dip her paint brushes into, and hooked her foot around a leg of her stool to pull it between the twin wheelchairs. She perched lightly on the edge of stool and studied Jess's eyes, wondering if she was doing the right thing.

Then she dipped the sponge into the water, squeezed out the excess, and trailed it lightly across Jess's cheek, the bridge of her nose, and along her jaw.

Jess's eyes registered surprise at first and then connection. She liked the feel of the damp sponge on her face. She liked that Cory was reaching out to her. Her eyes told Cory that she felt settled, better than she had felt before.

Cory repeated the procedure on Thomas. She didn't know if he felt it, or if he liked it or not. She couldn't ask and he couldn't answer.

Although she was quiet, Cory sensed when Melissa returned from the bathroom. She felt herself being watched interacting with her charges.

"Cory, thank you for taking care of them for me," Melissa said.

Cory's eyes slid toward Melissa before she nodded her acknowledgment.

"I am really impressed with how you wanted to share with them." She paused as if waiting for Cory to say something.

"Well, anyway, Cory, I am going to let your counselor know what happened today. I think it might be good for you to do a little more. Maybe you can get some sort of job or something. I am sure, under the right circumstances, you could handle it."

Cory sensed that Melissa was trying to be complimentary, but she didn't like the way she said, "under the right circumstances." There was something about that statement that made her feel like a lost cause and she didn't like it.

She shrugged her shoulders, turned her attention to her easel, and started to work in her own artistic bubble.

By the end of the day, Cory had almost completed the painting she started that morning. To her, the painting was like two sides of a coin. Two things that were opposite, but needed each other to exist in their own right.

Embellish

She was pleased with her work, and even more pleased that she had spent the entire day in the art room uninterrupted. It wasn't something that happened often, but it was wonderful when it did. Everyone in the school had forgotten about her. Nobody had checked on her for hours.

She had the chance to paint all day on the days when she was forgotten and nobody came to escort her to class or the cafeteria. It was easy for people to forget about the strange silent girl that kept to herself. She was, of course, perfectly capable of getting herself to different classes on time, but they didn't know that. Because she didn't want to leave the art room, she left it up to the school to find her and escort her to her where they wanted her to be. She always did what they told her to do, but she wouldn't initiate it if they forgot.

CHAPTER 3

Days later, Cory frowned into the mirror positioned next to her easel. She was working on a self-portrait. She was trying to paint an image of strength with herself as the model. It wasn't coming out right. Her neck was too long, her features too demure. She wanted to appear fearless in the painting and every time she reworked the image, she felt like it looked like a broken person in need of a protector. It was not the image she was going for and she couldn't seem to do anything to salvage it.

She groaned and covered her eyes with the palms of her hands considering ripping the paper out of its clamps and tearing it to shreds.

After reigning in her emotions, she decided instead she would clean up for the day. Maybe she would go home and not think about art for the afternoon. Maybe she would take a walk or listen to music. Maybe if she did something new, she'd have new images to paint.

She couldn't shake the frustrated feeling in her chest as she washed her paintbrushes in the sink. She was thinking about what she could do to repaint her portrait, to make it strong maybe even foreboding. Something that made her portrait look how she wanted to feel on the inside. It was challenging because it wasn't how she actually felt. Ever.

Her thoughts were interrupted by a quiet cough from across the room. Cory whirled on her heel toward the source of the sound. It was Mr. Winter, the school counselor.

"Cory, could you finish putting your things away and then come join me for a planning meeting."

Planning meeting. Cory hated the way the words made it sound like she had a choice in what would happen to her. She hated the way he made it seem like her future was a consensual, collaborative decision. It wasn't, but part of his job was to meet with her to talk about her future. She wasn't sure why he insisted on her showing up. Her presence served no actual purpose. In the meetings, he would talk to her, then write out what he talked about on a blue form. The form would be copied and sent to the state agency overseeing her case while the copy sat in a file in the thick chart he kept in the locked cabinet in his office next to his desk.

She shuddered to think about the contents of her file. Meeting after pointless meeting had been documented and filed away. They had them about once a month or maybe every six weeks. Sometimes her mother would join them. Sometimes she wouldn't. It didn't matter. The meetings were all basically the same anyway. Nothing really changed. She'd stay at the school, then would go to a group home when she turned twenty-one. That was her life. That was it and for some reason, Mr. Winter had to write it down on a blue form every single month. She wondered if he hated his job as much as she hated it for him.

She pursed her lips and squinted her eyes, trying to remember when her last meeting was. She felt like it was fairly recent. It certainly hadn't been a month ago already, had it?

She supposed it didn't matter. She was done painting for the day anyway. She had nothing better to do. Maybe it had been a month already and she was due for her meeting. It wasn't like she cared, besides he was the one who had to made sure all the right paperwork was done to keep her in the school that let her spend most of her time with her art.

Mr. Winter didn't bother trying to make conversation as they walked in silence down the hallway. He had tried many times over the years to get her to talk. She suspected he was dying to be able to say he was the hero that got the mute girl to open her mouth, but she wasn't about to make his dreams come true.

His shoes squeaked with every step down the long hall. Cory wondered how he could stand to wear squeaky shoes and if he ever tried to quiet the squeak when he stepped. She guessed he didn't. She wondered if he minded the noise at all. He seemed like the type of man who wouldn't notice.

As she walked she pulled out the rubber band holding her ponytail. It felt too tight and was giving her a headache. She fluffed her hair and absently rubbed her scalp, then swept the matted black locks forward over her shoulder. With effort, she separated the mass into three semi-even bunches and haphazardly braided it to keep it out of her face.

He led the way into the small conference room by the front office. She was surprised to see her mother and Principal Haddock already sitting around the table. They smiled at her when she entered the room. She felt immediately on edge. While her mother was occasionally present at their meetings, the principal had never once joined them.

Mr. Winter gestured for her to sit as he pulled out the chair next to her mother for himself. "Thank you for joining us." He acknowledged her mother and the principal with a curt nod.

Cory was confused about the meeting. She had never been to one as formal. She stared at her mother, willing her to understand that she wanted to know what the meeting was about. She wanted her mother to answer her wordless questions. She felt a sense of anxiety building in her chest.

Mr. Winter sat looking pleased before he cleared his throat and said, "I called this meeting today because I thought we might need to revise our game plan for Cory."

Cory's eyes opened wide, a sense of foreboding crept through her.

"It has recently come to our attention that Cory might be in need of more..." Mr. Winter paused as he searched for the right word. She hated the note of self-importance in his voice. "More stimulation. Not that you aren't doing well." He smiled kindly at her, "but I think we might have been underestimating you, Miss Fall."

Cory's head spun. She wanted to be underestimated. It was what she strived for. She wanted to be ignored. She wanted to scream at them to leave her alone and not change anything about her life, but she said nothing.

Principal Haddock seemed to sense Cory's inner turmoil, "Cory, there have been a few recent developments that might change what you can do in your future and I think we owe it to you to explore them."

Cory shook her head in a minute no. She didn't want anything to change. She was happy with things the way things were and with her future plans.

"Now, Cory," Principal Haddock went on in a softer voice that she supposed was meant to sound understanding, "we have noticed how you interact with some of the other kids, especially the kids with significant needs. You are good with them, and perhaps you can do more with that."

Cory said nothing as she kept her face in a neutral mask, willing Principal Haddock to continue.

"We also had some interest in your paintings."

That caught Cory off-guard. Her expression slipped into one of surprise.

Principal Haddock and her mother exchanged small glances that suggested they had been working together on something.

"Cory, honey, Principal Haddock called me a few months ago about your paintings. There have been so many of them, she wanted to know what to do with them. I didn't know, we have so many at home, you know." Her mother's voice trailed off in contemplation.

"So, we called around and Rimrock Mall had some space where they showcase local art. We brought yours and had an exhibition from the school. Your work was prominently featured. It has brought a lot of positive publicity."

Horrified was the only emotion Cory felt as she listened to the discussion.

"Anyway," her mother continued in a hurry after she caught sight of the expression that crossed her daughter's face, "people liked your work. Several called the school to tell them how impressed they were, honey."

Cori felt like growling. It was just what she didn't want, people calling the school telling them they were impressed that the special girl at the special school was able to hold a paintbrush to paper and create something, something special.

Her mind flashed to the article she read about on the Internet a while back where a gorilla at a zoo drew pictures with crayons. The pictures looked like something a toddler would scribble, but they were hot commodities at the zoo gift shop. Of course, he ate the crayons when he was done with them, he was a gorilla after all. And she was the special girl at the special school that would one day grow up to live in the group home.

She wanted to scream. She hadn't realized how much her life was like the gorilla at the zoo.

She felt tears prickle in her eyes. She couldn't let them fall. She bit the inside of her cheek and shifted her gaze to the ceiling, just like Thomas. She couldn't let anybody see how she felt. She wouldn't let anybody in.

"So," Mr. Winters went on, having no idea about the inner turmoil going through Cory. "We thought we should revise your plan and look at helping you get a job."

He looked pleased with himself. Principal Haddock looked encouraging. Her mother looked nervous.

"We'd like to have you work outside of the school, in order to help prepare you for when you graduate. We thought you could help out with the art classes for special needs adults at the community center. It would be four hours a week and you would get paid."

He looked like he expected Cory to be grateful for his successful efforts in securing her a job.

It wasn't that Cory didn't want to help with the classes, that part actually sounded like something she would enjoy. What she just didn't want was to believe she was so defective that the only thing she could hope for was a four-hour a week job at a community art center. She felt so hopeless and out of control. It wasn't that she ever thought of having a job before the meeting. She hadn't considered doing anything but her art, but now that she knew employment might be expected of her, she wished she could be in charge of it. Her options were so minimal, she felt like crying for herself.

Mr. Winters finally recognized that Cory was having conflicting emotions. He thought she might be worried about doing the work. Trying to be helpful, he added, "it will work out beautifully, I know it will. We will have a classroom aid go with you the whole time you are at work to make sure you are doing okay."

She'd have an aid with her at work. At her four-hour a week job. Nobody thought she was capable enough to help at an art class by herself. Of course, she reasoned, why would they think she was capable? She never gave any indication that she could do... anything.

Cory gave up trying to hold back the tears. She felt them stream in earnest down her face. Before anyone could say anything else, she stood and ran as fast as she could back to the solace of the art room.

CHAPTER 4

The first thing she did was pull her previous self-portrait out of the easel clips and toss it unceremoniously into the garbage. There was nothing right about the portrait. It wasn't her and as of now, she had deemed it unsalvageable. She put up a fresh sheet, larger than the first. Then went to the supply closet at the back of the room looking for a box of charcoal pastels.

She didn't work with charcoal very often, but today it felt right. She picked up a newish piece of the square chalk and started to draw. It was another self-portrait, but this time she didn't bother looking in the mirror. She worked off of feelings and memory.

Her hand hurriedly swept across the paper in broad, sure, angry strokes.

Cory didn't look up when she heard the sound of her mother's heels entering the room, followed by the sound of a stool being pulled across the linoleum. She figured her mom planned to sit and watch her work. Cory wondered if her mom wanted her to get a job. She wondered if her mom thought she was capable. She always suspected that her mother always thought she was too fragile to be alone in the outside world. If there was one thing she could count on, it was her mother always being there for her. She never had to worry because her mom always did everything for her.

Cory's loved her mom and the way things were, but she couldn't help but wonder what it would be like if she made some of her own decisions.

The meeting had been too much for her and she needed the release that her art gave her. Cory pushed aside her thoughts about her mother, her life, and her lack of decisions. She needed to focus and work on her art. She needed to lose herself.

Cory worked with a frenzied energy and soon forgot she was at school and that her mother sat watching. Although, she probably wouldn't have stopped even if she remembered there was an audience.

The woman that emerged on her paper had broad, bare shoulders, feminine yet strong. The neck was thicker than Cory's, the jaw a little more squared, the lips were thinner, but the girl in the portrait was undeniably Cory. There was a defiant look in the portrait girl's eye. Cory continued to refine, sketching and blending the hair and skin with skilled fingers so they looked like they were alive.

The girl in the portrait was strength. She was control, courage, and anger. There could be no doubt that she was a warrior. She was everything Cory wanted to be.

As she studied the drawing, fresh tears poured down Cory's cheeks as her hands swept back and forth across the paper. She wondered why she couldn't just be normal. She knew she didn't have to be a warrior. She just wanted to stop being a misfit among misfits.

Her mother stepped forward and put an arm around Cory's thin shoulders. At five feet eight inches, her mother was tall, but not as tall as Cory. Cory was a good three inches taller than her mother, but she curled against her body, made herself small, and leaned her head on her shoulder. She wanted to be held like a small child. She wanted comfort. She needed her mother to hold her, love her, and tell her everything would be alright.

"Cory, honey, are you going to be okay?" Her mother cooed as if she could read her thoughts. "Cory, I will take care of you just like always, okay? You don't have to do anything you don't want to do. I am here for you. You can get a job or not get a job. I just want you to focus on you, okay, honey?"

Cory felt comforted by the gentle support. Her mother said exactly what she wanted to hear. She didn't want to have to face reality. She didn't want to feel like a faceless adult. She wanted to be herself, do her art, and just exist. If it meant she would have to live a supervised life, so be it. She didn't care. It didn't matter to her anyway.

Cory stood and allowed herself to be cocooned in her mother's arms.

"Your drawing is impressive, honey," her mother praised after studying the charcoal for several minutes. "I love seeing you without the makeup all the time even if it is a portrait. Sometimes, I just miss your beautiful face."

Cory said nothing. She supposed mothers had to say their daughters had a beautiful face no matter what they looked like. She had been a child model, she had been beautiful. But now, she did everything she could to conceal herself. Cory said nothing out loud. There wasn't anything to say.

"Come on, honey. Let's get you home. I will make you some dinner and you can go paint a little before bed. That sounds good doesn't it, sweetie?"

Cory didn't nod in agreement, but it did sound good. She simply picked up her bag and hoisted it onto her thin shoulder. She looked at her soot-black hands covered in charcoal and considered washing them.

"Cory, you need to wash your hands, baby. The sink is right over there. The soap is by the faucet. Please wash your hands, honey. Then we can go home."

Cory moved to the sink with heavy, zombielike steps and washed her hands. Her mother had taken charge and she was a willing follower.

CHAPTER 5

Cory dozed off in the car on the way home and woke when she felt the car stop in the driveway. She heard the keys jangle as her mother pulled them out of the ignition and threw them into her purse. Her mother's cool fingers slid gently from her temple to her jaw and she felt comforted like she didn't need to worry about anything anymore. From that simple touch, she was reassured her mother would always take care of her.

"Come on, honey. Let's go inside. You can shower and I will make you some dinner, okay?" Her mother spoke quietly.

Cory looked into her mother's teal eyes, the exact shade of her own, and saw nothing but love and concern. If there was one thing she never doubted, it was her mother's complete love and devotion. Her mother had always been there for her.

She mindlessly stumbled into the house, up the stairs, and into the bathroom just off her bedroom. She turned on the water to the shower to let the water warm as she stripped out of her clothes.

By the time she stepped in, the water was hot. It scalded her skin, but she didn't move or flinch away. She merely watched as black from the charcoal streamed off her hands and forearms down her legs toward the drain. She took the white bar of soap and rubbed it in between her hands. It turned black in her palms. She rinsed it until the bubbles on the bar and her hands were clear. She repeated the process across her body until she and the soap were clean. After that, she took a washcloth and scrubbed at her face until it felt raw and free of all traces of makeup.

She didn't bother washing her hair. It was so long and thick, she didn't want to have to work the shampoo and conditioner into it only to go to the trouble of rinsing. Maybe, she thought, she didn't need hair anymore. It didn't serve much of a purpose and a shaved head would certainly be easier to deal with.

She vowed to sometime soon consider the merits of going bald.

She shut off the water, wrapped one towel around her hair and another around her body. Then she sat on her bed and waited as if in a trance for something to happen.

Eventually, her mother knocked on her door, let herself in, and told her dinner was ready. She glanced at Cory. Noticing her towel, she went to the dresser and pulled out a pair of panties, black leggings, and an oversized black sweatshirt. She knew her mother would have preferred color in Cory's wardrobe, but there wasn't any. Cory preferred black.

"You need to get dressed, honey. Here are some clothes for you. Can you do it yourself or do you need me to help you?" The tone of her voice sounded like someone asking a small child if they needed help, not a teen who was almost technically a legal adult.

But then again, that is how it was for them. Her mother did everything for her. It had always been this way, at least since she had gotten out of the hospital when she was eight. It was a pattern they fell into. Her mother took charge of everything, and Cory let her. Cory didn't have to think or feel or do anything. She could be cared for. She knew her mother felt an overwhelming need to be everything for her. It bothered her that her mother was always trying to make up for not being there that day. Cory assumed her mom felt guilty for everything that had happened, even though none of it had anything to do with her and everything to do with him. He was the one that caused their pain when he tried his best to kill her.

But Cory had forgiven her father long ago and never did blame her mother. She wished she could set her mom free by telling her it wasn't her fault that she was the way she was. She wished her mom didn't feel responsible for what happened, but she couldn't form the words to tell her and writing it down seemed too impersonal. Although she reasoned, it didn't really matter, her mother would never believe her. She would always blame herself. It was who she was.

In Cory's mind, her mother's only fault was that she loved her dad at one time. At least she loved him long enough to get pregnant with her. If she hadn't, Cory wouldn't have been born at all.

Maybe, Cory wondered, her mother was at fault. Maybe she shouldn't have been born. If her mother had never been swept away by her father's fraudulent charms, none of them would have ever known the pain they had been through. Her mother could have been something if she didn't have to watch over her so much.

Cory swallowed hard and forced herself to get dressed. She moved like she was swimming through thickening concrete. She made her way to the kitchen, but she didn't want to eat dinner. She didn't feel like it. She didn't think she'd be able to swallow food that she put in her mouth. She didn't want her mother telling every step she needed to take. She wanted to be free to make her own decisions. She didn't want to think about working a job four hours a week under the supervision of a classroom aid or her future living in a group home. She didn't want to wonder if her art was only interesting to others because it was a curiosity made by a freak.

She needed to stop thinking and lose herself

tonight. The best way to stop her mind's internal chatter was to completely focus on her art. It made time stand still and everything that bothered her fade away.

After washing the dishes, Cory went to her room and looked at her bedroom walls. They were covered with paintings unconnected to each other. Some were so large they were almost murals, others were so small they looked like illustrations in an old book. Together, they looked like graffiti under a bridge, so many opposing pieces done in clashing styles, many varying thoughts and feelings expressed. They were all so different, but when they were viewed together on her walls, they looked like a single cohesive image.

On top of her desk, she had a plastic container with a lid. She popped the lid open to expose her wet paints. She took a brush from a mug full of brushes on top of her dresser. She sat on her knees near the left edge of her window and started to lose herself. She wasn't sure what she was going to paint, she was going to see what came to her as she covered the previous image in its place.

Cory was unaware that while she was busy forgetting herself in her art, her mom sat alone at the kitchen table quietly crying for the smiling, vibrant daughter she lost at the age of 8 and for her silent, haunted daughter upstairs lost in her own head.

CHAPTER 6

She stayed up late painting a dragon coiling and twisting its body down her window frame. With a fine brush, she created colorfully muted scales in blues, purples, and grays. They reminded her of oil slicks in puddles after the rain. The dragon's eyes were appraising. It had obvious power but remained passive in its stillness.

She hadn't done a great job cleaning up last night before crawling to her bed and pulling up the covers in exhaustion. Her paintbrushes sat next to the sink, mostly clean, but not completely. At least she recovered her paint in plastic before falling asleep. She hadn't noticed the blobs of green and blue paint now dry on her carpet near the window. She saw them clearly in the morning light. She sighed. She hated that she had carpet in the room, but neither she nor her mom bothered trying to clean it anymore. At this point, they figured it would be better to simply re-carpet when they were ready to move out of the house.

Cory gave a halfhearted attempt at cleaning the paint off her hands and forearms. She picked at some dried paint on her forearms. Since she knew it would eventually come off, she gave up quickly. Clean skin wasn't worth the effort when she would be staining it again as soon as she could.

She applied her makeup and peeked out the window. It looked cold and drizzly. She pulled a thick shapeless black sweater over the shirt she slept in, then tugged a short black skirt over her black leggings before pulling on her black combat boots.

It was Saturday and she hoped her mom would take her to the art store for supplies. She was surprised it was almost lunchtime. She didn't realize how late she'd slept in.

There was a note on the kitchen table from her mom telling her she had errands to run.

Cory cursed herself in her mind. She should have gotten up earlier so she could have had a ride to the art store.

The day was so cold and gray. It was the perfect day to stay inside, drink tea, and paint. Unfortunately, the art store would be closed on Sunday. She had to go today.

Her mom didn't like her to go out of the house by herself, but Cory knew the way. She didn't need her mom to take her to the store. She could walk there by herself. Couldn't she?

She drank some juice and ate a piece of toast before pulling open the cookie jar. She and her mom kept cash in the cookie jar for days like today. She really needed to go today or she would be out of luck until Monday at the earliest.

Cory considered how long it would take her to get there and back. She wondered how her long her mom would be gone. She wasn't sure how many errands she had to run or if she could get back to the house before her mom. Then she wondered if it mattered. Her mother would be upset, but Cory knew she could do it. The art store wasn't that far away. Maybe it would be good for her mom to see her as capable.

She recalled the gorilla painting in the zoo and how much its life was going to be like hers in the group home.

Her cheeks flushed. She loved to be ignored and allowed to paint, but she would love it even more if she could do it on her own. She knew she wouldn't be able to do everything herself, but she would love it if she could do a little more.

Filled with a fledgling sense of purpose, she picked up a pen and scrawled at the bottom of her mom's note that she was going to go for a walk. She could have texted, but she liked the idea that she might beat her mom home and, in doing so, keep her from being worried. Plus, she didn't want to run the risk that her mother would tell her she wasn't allowed to go at all. She pulled out two twenties and shoved them into a zippered pocket of her backpack.

Her walk was long and cold. She felt her heavy eye makeup burning as it ran into her eyes and down onto her cheeks, but she didn't mind. She wasn't going to try to stop it. She figured she would draw herself with her running makeup when she got home. It could make an interesting self-portrait.

The bell at the top of the door chimed as she opened it, alerting the shop owner, Gavin Forrest, of her presence.

"Hey Cory," he yelled when he saw who it was. He didn't expect her to answer. He had known her and her mother for years, they were excellent customers.

Cory acknowledged Gavin with a small finger wave and then set about her task of methodically walking up and down the aisle gathering what she needed. She had a mental list and an empty backpack to carry home her treasures.

She didn't notice the tall boy with dark brown, caramel colored hair, light brown skin, and pale blue eyes holding a stack flyers he hoped to post in the art store. She didn't realize she looked like an intimidating gothic mess, but also somehow fragile at the same time. She didn't see the boy's eyes glued to her as she moved purposefully through the store.

Normally she would have taken her time looking at supplies, but today she was in a hurry to get home. She didn't want her mom to come home and worry about her absence. As she shopped, she caught sight of her reflection in the large round mirror positioned for Gavin to spot shoplifters from where he sat by the cash register. She thought she looked like the evil character in a horror movie. She was so wet she looked like she was melting. Her makeup had indeed run from her eyes, down her cheeks, and down into the neck of her sweater. Her hair hung like dead snakes down her back. She couldn't help but smile at the ridiculousness of her image. How could anyone go out looking the way she was now, especially if they wanted to blend in?

Her smile faded as she finally noticed the tall boy in a vintage rock and roll t-shirt, an unzipped gray sweatshirt, and a pair of dark skinny jeans looking at her. He was handsome and seemed to be smiling in response to her smile like they were sharing some sort of inside joke. He made a move to walk toward like he wanted to engage her in conversation.

Cory felt sweat instantly rise to the surface of her skin. Alarm bells began to sound in her head. She had the overwhelming urge to run out of the store. She quickly turned on her heel to take her supplies to the cash register. She had most of what she had come for. Everything else could wait.

Gavin began ringing her up, speaking with her as if they were having a mundane conversation that wasn't one-sided. It was what he always did when she came to the store.

The boy made his way to the register as well. He stood too close to the counter for someone waiting their turn in line. Out of her peripheral vision, she saw him trying unsuccessfully to catch her eye. It was like he needed to talk to her and couldn't let her get away. He made her nervous. He seemed intent on engaging her in conversation. She didn't talk, couldn't talk. She had to get away.

He reached out toward her as if he was going to touch her arm. He looked like he wanted to introduce himself. She knew if he did, they would stand awkwardly waiting for something that would never happen. She needed to leave.

She ignored the boy, paid quickly, and practically sprinted from the store as soon as the bag and the receipt were in her hand. On the way home, she tried to figure out why she had such an intense reaction. She had seen boys before, some were even cute, but this boy freaked her out. Maybe it was the way he seemed intent on trying to engage her. Since she had no experience with boys or talking, it made her panic.

She had to admit there was a part of her that would have liked to talk to him. She wished she was normal and could have a conversation with a cute boy in an art store. She wished she could flip a switch in her mind and be normal, but she couldn't. She didn't know how. She wasn't someone who could have a relationship no matter how much she might want one. It simply wasn't an option.

She listened to the gentle splats of rain and tried to distract herself with thoughts of her next painting as she walked home.

She half expected her mom to be pacing at the door when she got back. It was cold and rainy, not the kind of day to run errands or walk to an art store. It was the kind of day that demanded blankets on the couch and long naps. At least they would both have their errands done and would be able to stay in for the rest of the day.

Cory took off her boots by the front door. She set her supplies carefully down on the coffee table and then started up the stairs stripping off layers of wet clothes while she went. Before she did anything else, she needed a hot shower.

It took a long time for the water to do its job and take the chill off her skin. Finally feeling revitalized she dried her hair and pulled on a fleece sweatshirt, leggings, and fuzzy socks. She put her wet clothes in the wash and went to look for her mother.

She peeked into her room, the kitchen, and the living room before looking outside for her car. The day had gotten worse. It was now pouring rain and looked like night, even though it was early afternoon. She was surprised her mother wasn't back yet, but since she didn't know what her mom had planned she didn't worry.

She looked in the refrigerator thinking she should get something to eat. She poked through the shelves, but nothing looked good. She considered crackers from the pantry but didn't find any. Maybe one of her mother's errands was grocery shopping. Cory decided to wait until her mom got home to eat, maybe she would have better options after she got home.

She went to her room to wait. She propped the pillows on her bed so she could lean against the wall with an oversized sketchbook on her lap. She wanted to let her mind wander and draw. She hoped she'd get ideas for her next painting. She hadn't been inspired on her way home.

As she sketched, a figure emerged on the paper in front of her. He was tall with the right amount of muscles. His face was open and smiling, he was handsome the way his slightly long hair fringed his face, his gorgeous eyes crinkling slightly at the corner. She knew the boy she was randomly drawing. It was the boy from the art store, the one she had run away from.

Abruptly, she shut her sketchbook and threw it on the floor next to her bed. She shoved the pencil into the back of her ponytail, sighing in frustration, she leaned against her pillows. Why did she have to be the way she was? Why couldn't she just open her mouth and talk? Why couldn't she go places by herself and be a normal teenager? Why did she have to hide in her room and fill her time with her art?

Why couldn't she be different?

CHAPTER 7

She pointed her toes and straightened her legs before reaching her hands overhead into a full body stretch when she woke. She squeezed her eyes shut before blinking them open. She hadn't meant to fall asleep, but her bed felt so warm and secure. It had been cold outside, it was the kind of day that made a person need to crawl under the covers and give up on reality for at least a little while.

Becoming more fully awake every second, she glanced at the clock and was surprised at the time. It was getting close to dinner, and for some reason, she didn't hear sounds of cooking or smell anything being made in the kitchen.

Her mom loved to cook and they almost always had dinner together. Maybe, she thought, her mom had different plans. They hadn't touched base that morning, there could be something one or both of them needed to do.

Cory hoped her mom didn't have any plans that included her. She didn't want to go out. She didn't want to have to put on her makeup and dress in her layers of clothes. She didn't want to have anyone on the outside stare at her and wonder why she looked the way she did. She just wanted to stay home and paint with her new supplies. She wanted to stay home and do the same thing she always did.

Forcing herself to stand at the side of her bed, she stretched again before making her way downstairs.

It was strange that the house was empty. Her mom's car still wasn't parked in its spot. She wondered if her mom had been home and then left again. Had she tried to wake her? She didn't think so, but maybe she'd been sleeping so soundly she missed something. Cory pulled her eyebrows together while her mouth twisted into a frown.

She padded her way to the kitchen where she found her mom's note about errands and her own addition about going out. There was nothing after that from her mom. Maybe, Cory thought, she hadn't been back at all.

It was strange for her mother to be gone all day. She felt the beginnings of a twinge of worry start to nag in her chest. Cory did her best to ignore the feeling and reassure herself that her mother was fine. She was probably just busy and didn't realize the time.

She dug her phone out of her backpack to check for messages. Of course, it was dead. She plugged it and waited impatiently for it to charge enough to turn it on.

There were no texts or voicemails waiting for her. She sent a quick text asking where she was.

She stared at the phone for a minute, but her mom never was quick to respond to texts. She told herself that her mom would come rushing in any minute with some story of how she got caught up in the unexpected. She would apologize profusely for leaving Cory alone all day and then she would look Cory over, make her too much food, and fuss around making sure everything was ready for the next day. Cory smiled at the thought of her ultraprotective mother. She could picture it all so clearly, it almost seemed real in her mind.

She made herself a grilled cheese sandwich and a glass of milk and ate slowly. Her eyes were fixed on the door. She was waiting for her mom to come flying in the door at any moment. Then they would spend some time together before bed. Her mom surely had some sort of tale to tell about her day. It had happened several times before.

Cory finished her dinner but continued to sit patiently. Her mom never did burst through the door.

Eventually, she sighed, loaded her dishes into the dishwasher, straightened the kitchen and living room, and then made her way back to her bedroom.

She took her time setting up her easel and paints. Still expecting her mother to be home any second, she was hesitant to start because she didn't want to get everything out only to have to put it away again minutes later when her mom got home.

But she didn't come, so Cory turned on her music and got to work.

That was one thing about art. When she was working, everything else fell away. She didn't consciously worry about anything, even though she could see her feeling come alive in her canvases as she worked. She was certain there was a part of her brain that only fired when she was painting. When she was lost in her work, hours passed without her realizing. She was only concerned with line and color and how the image made her feel.

Because of her afternoon nap, it was four in the morning before Cory washed and fell into bed with heavy eyes and a desire for sleep.

CHAPTER 8

She felt like she hadn't slept at all when the doorbell rang.

The doorbell rang again.

Cory wanted to ignore it. She rolled over in bed and pulled the pillow over her ears. Her mom would get answer it anyway. She always did. She burrowed further under the covers.

As she snuggled herself into bed, her thoughts slowly started to focus. Recollection began to fill her mind. Yesterday, her mother didn't come home. She didn't call or text. There had been nothing. Her mother had left her before to do errands, but she had always been home by bedtime at the latest. Something had to be wrong.

Heavy panic surged through her body like molten lead.

The doorbell rang a third time.

This time she jumped from her bed, pulled on her robe and ran as fast as she could down the stairs. She missed the last step and almost crashed into the wall at the bottom of the stairs.

Out of breath, she hurriedly unlocked the deadbolt and yanked the door open just in time to see the two police officers walking toward the cruiser parked in front of her house.

Cory was sure her heart stopped. She knew what police meant. The last time they had come to see her was when she was recovering in the rehab hospital. They asked her question after question that she never answered about her dad. Eventually, they stopped coming, they stopped trying to talk to her, until today.

Tears started prickling in her eyes. She didn't want

to hear anything that they had to say, even though her heart was telling her she had to listen.

She rearranged her face into a stoic mask, hiding her overwhelming feeling of fear and fighting the urge to scream. She wanted to beg for her mother to be okay, but she said nothing. She simply opened the door wider, gesturing for the officers to come in.

Wordlessly, they clomped into her living room and found positions next to each other on the couch in the living room while Cory sat gingerly across from them in the recliner. Her blood felt like ice. She knew what they were going to say. She wished they would get on with it and get out of her house. She needed to be free to fall apart on her own.

"Are you Cory Fall?" Asked the older officer with the balding head and kind dark eyes.

She nodded.

"I am Officer Whelan. This is Officer Shelby. We are so sorry we have to tell you this." He started, but then faltered as he took in her trembling hands and waifish appearance. "Is there someone else we can call for you right now. Maybe your father could come over?"

Cory vehemently shook her head no, silently begging with her eyes for him to continue.

Officer Whelan acknowledged her with a small nod of his head before he continued to explain about her mother's accident. She had lost control of her car at the bend in the road. It slid down a muddy embankment before crashing into a tree at the bottom of the hill. Because of the rain, nobody noticed the crash for several hours.

Cory listened intently as the officer confirmed what she already knew to be true. Her mother was gone. Her mother, who loved her, shielded her and did everything for her was gone. She felt her stomach lurch and for a moment she thought she would vomit right there in front of the officers.

She tried to hold herself together even though she knew with certainty that she was falling apart. She wanted to let everything out by howling her pain. But she didn't. She stood stoically, expertly holding herself together in complete silence. She needed the whole story, and the officer seemed willing to provide it. She held herself still and listened.

"She hit her head on the steering wheel. She was gone instantly." He said in a soft consoling voice.

She felt the edges of her world begin to crumble. Instead of crying or screaming her pain, she went numb. She stopped trying to listen to the officers as they described the recovery efforts. On some level, she registered them saying that everything had taken so long because of the weather. They had to make sure conditions were safe for the rescuers.

Cory closed her eyes, willing the officers to disappear along with her pain. She tried to imagine her mother's arms gently circling her shoulders. She needed her mother holding her.

She opened her eyes just in time to see the look the officers gave each other and knew exactly what it meant. She figured they had been the bearers of bad news many times over the years. Their look said they knew how people reacted to bad news and she wasn't doing it right. She knew the officers would not leave her alone in her grief. They were going to try to figure out what was wrong with her.

Officer Shelby silently snuck out of the house to the cruiser to make some phone calls while Officer Whelan tried to comfort Cory.

A short time later, Officer Shelby returned. She nodded to Officer Whelan in another silent communication before quietly stating in what seemed to be an attempt at a soothing tone, "Cory, your caseworker, Abigail Mitchum, will be here soon. We were lucky she was on call this weekend."

Officer Whelan's eyes shot to his partner, obviously surprised Cory had a caseworker and probably wondering why she needed one.

Cory had known Abigail since she was 8 years-old. Cory didn't like the way Abigail always called her by her full name, Corrina. Still, she was the one who had helped her get placed at her school. She worked with Mr. Winters to follow her progress and stay in the loop with her future plans. Abigail had even mentioned helping Cory sell some of her work so she'd have enough spending money to keep her in supplies in the future. Cory knew she did more for her than she technically had to. As a thank you, she occasionally gave her paintings.

Cory didn't want to think about Abigail or her future. She felt like she was drowning and she couldn't breathe. She needed her mom. She had no idea what was she supposed to do.

She pulled her knees to her chest, folded her head into her arms, and started to cry

.

CHAPTER 9

She wasn't sure how long she cried. At one point, one of the officers handed her tissues and then a wet washcloth.

Eventually, she had nothing left and sat in numb silence. She could tell the officers were uncomfortable with her lack of communication. They tried to soothe her with kind words, but she didn't respond. The silence was broken only by occasional tweets of the cell phones attached to their belts on the other side of their guns.

Cory stared at her front door, willing her mother to walk through it. She tried to envision her mother blowing in with a smile and a giggle ready to tell her all about the crazy day she had. Then she would tell the officers that there had been some sort of mix-up and it wasn't her car that crashed. Or maybe she would tell them that she loaned her car to someone else and she had only just now been able to get home. It was someone else who died. It had to be, Cory told herself. It was some faceless, nameless person who had borrowed her mother's car. That person had no friends or family to mourn them. They wouldn't be missed. Even in her fantasy's she wouldn't let another person feel the loss she was feeling now.

Cory desperately wished the accident happening to someone else was the truth. She would do anything to bring her mom back. There had to have been a mistake. Somehow her mother would still be coming home. Maybe there wasn't even a car crash at all. Maybe, if there was a crash, her mother wasn't in the car. Maybe there was a mix-up in the identity of the person at the hospital. Maybe her mother was actually in the hospital in a coma, unable to speak, unable to say who she was.

She felt her body closing in on itself. Like she was a piece of origami paper being folded and folded again, disappearing into something unrecognizable. Her vision blurred. Her body felt like it was floating, unattached to anything in the room around her. She wanted to pretend she was still in bed, halfway between sleep and reality, where dreams seem real but aren't. She wanted nothing more than to pop her eyes open, find herself snuggled in her bed, and realize that this morning had been nothing more than a horrible nightmare.

She had almost convinced herself that she was dreaming and that she could force herself awake when a soft rapping interrupted her thoughts.

She stood and floated to the door as if she was in a trance.

Standing at the threshold was Abigail Mitchum.

"Corrina, honey," Abigail said as she took two steps into the house. Her arms extended open, ready to offer an embrace.

Cory struggled to think why Abigail would be coming to her door on a Sunday morning. She didn't want a hug. She wanted her mom. Where was her mom?

Cory blinked. Her mind was fighting something. There was something real she didn't want to believe. She felt her mind trying to deny the truth of what happened. At the same time a small part of her that was trying to tell her that everything was real and she had to stay in the present. That small part of her brain was screaming at her to keep it together.

Cory felt her mind snap. The truth hit her again with full force. She couldn't deny what had happened. She couldn't believe there was a mix-up. She was fully awake. There were officers in her living room. Her caseworker just came to the door. She knew the truth. The horrible truth that her mother was gone and wouldn't be coming back.

She fell to her knees and let out a gut-wrenching howl. Abigail automatically sank down beside her letting her purse and bag of files fall to the floor. She pulled Cory into an awkward half hug and held her until her tears stopped.

Cory's eyes were heavy and aching after her cry. She didn't know what she was supposed to do next.

The officers stood and spoke quietly with Abigail for a few minutes before handing her their card. Abigail nodded at them in reassurance. Officer Whelan patted Cory's arm as he made his way out of the house. Officer Shelby offered her condolences and then they were gone.

Cory felt like she was in a bubble. Maybe a bubble that was underwater. She could hear when Abigail or the officers talked, but their voices were distorted and she was having trouble understanding their words. Her heart was shattered. She needed her mother to hold her and help her know what was coming next.

She felt Abigail 's cold fingers pull at her wrist. She led her to the couch and then tugged her hand for her to sit.

"Corrina," she started to say, "I am so sorry for your loss. I hate to have to do this right now. I can't imagine what you are going through, but I have to make sure you are safe." She paused as if waiting for Cory to say something, even though they both knew that wouldn't happen.

"Corrina, we will be considering permanent options for you, but for now we need to get you settled in an emergency placement."

Cory's mouth dropped open. It hadn't yet crossed

her mind that she wouldn't be able to stay at her home, but she wanted to. She knew she would be fine. She couldn't go somewhere else. Not now, especially not now.

She shook her head vehemently from side to side. She could not leave her house.

Abigail gently placed her hand on Cory's knee. "Now, Corrina, please hear me out. Let me talk to you about the options we have okay."

Cory closed her eyes and took a deep breath trying to calm her mind and slow her thundering heart.

"I know you, Corrina. I know what kind of person you are. I know what kind of things you need. Unfortunately, you are only sixteen years old. There is no way, you will be allowed to stay here alone at this time." Abigail pursed her lips closed, waiting for a reaction from Cory. Surprisingly, there wasn't one. Cory simply stared at her.

She continued, "I reviewed your file this morning. I know there really isn't anyone you are close to right now or who could step in for you today. There are no family members for us to contact, but I do remember your mom talking about her sister years ago when we first met. I don't have a number for her. It is going to take some time to track her down and then we can go from there."

Cory vaguely remembered her aunt Miranda. She looked a lot like her mom. She had curly dirty blond hair, a slim build, and teal colored eyes the same shade as her own. She hadn't thought about her aunt in ages. It had been years since she had seen her. There had been some sort of fight between her mom and her aunt and she hadn't seen her since.

Cory felt a wave of sadness wash over her. Her mom was gone and she had nobody. She was sure even if they could get ahold of her aunt, she would want nothing to do with her. She wiped at the tear that threatened to fall from her eye.

Abigail continued to murmur to herself and shuffle her papers in the file in front of her. "I made a couple of calls before I came here this morning. It can sometimes be a challenge to find emergency shelter for our older teens, especially for someone with special needs. I wanted to get the ball rolling as soon as possible. Right now, I am waiting for someone to call me back. Don't worry, we will get everything arranged. Why don't you go ahead and take a shower, maybe even pack a bag? That way we will be all ready to go when we find out where we need to be."

She had no idea what Abigail was talking about. She felt intensely confused, especially about the part about being special needs. It made her feel like some sort of reject. Yes, she went to a school for kids with issues, but did that mean she was special needs? She picked up Abigail 's pen and drew a large question mark on the front of one of her manila file folders.

Abigail paused and looked at Cory. Gently, she said, "you can't stay here by yourself, not after this kind of crisis. It is against all the rules. I am going to try to track down your aunt to find out more about your family. There might be someone that would be suitable for you to live with, but in the meantime, we need to find you some sort of short-term shelter."

Cory closed her eyes and slowly shook her head in disbelief. She had nobody she could turn to and ironically, she couldn't ask for help if she wanted to.

"I am going to find you the best possible place, okay. No matter where it is, you have to remember it will only be a little while. I will find you somewhere better for the long term." It was almost as if she was prepping Cory for a horrible situation. "I don't know if your aunt is suitable for a long-term placement, but if not, we will probably be looking for a group home of some sort and that won't be too bad. We have talked about a group home for you after you turned 21 anyway, remember?"

Cory did remember. The group home idea had always seemed so remote and vaguely unreal. It was an idea for her future self, but the future always seemed so far away and she never imagined it without her mom. She never worried about it before, but now that it was here, staring her in the face, the idea filled her with unease.

What did she want? Did she want to live with her aunt? She didn't want a group home, not now, she wasn't ready. At the same time, she didn't have a choice. She wanted to stay in her own house, at least tonight, she wanted to sleep in her mother's bed. She wanted to feel close to her at least for tonight.

Remembering Abigail's words to pack a bag and be ready to go, Cory stood to go to her room.

She found a duffle bag in the back of her closet. She had to pack a bag.

In it, she placed a box of charcoal pastels and a box of colored oil pastels. They weren't new boxes, but there was enough to get her through her immediate future. She added three different size notebooks with several blank pages left, some drawing pencils, a smudge stick, and a couple of well-used erasers. Then she wrapped a hairband around a handful of different size paint brushes before adding it to the bag with a set of oil paints and a set of watercolors. She thought that would do for however long she was gone. From her dresser, she added a haphazard assortment of panties, socks, a pair of pajama pants and a long sleeve t-shirt. She pulled a black cable sweater over her head and checked that the leggings she was wearing didn't have holes in the knees.

She didn't want a shower. Instead, she went to the bathroom to apply her face. She applied foundation before setting it with extra pale face powder. She outlined her lips and eyes in her thick black liner before sloppily smearing it at the edges around her eyes. Then she smoothed her black lipstick over her lips before packing her makeup, toothbrush, and toothpaste into her duffle bag.

She stood looking around her room, knowing she was leaving. Her life would never be the same again. She blinked her eyes and shifted her gaze to the ceiling, trying not to let tears spill out.

She needed to feel her mother near her.

She tiptoed out of the room and down the hall. She reverently entered her mother's room. She wanted to surround herself with her mother's things, smell her scent, and pretend her mother was near. She needed to cry.

She was about to let go when she heard Abigail call to her from downstairs. She said they found a placement and they would need to be going.

Cory felt like her solace was being ripped from her grasp. She needed to feel her mother, but she also had to leave her house. She had no idea when she would be able to come back.

She looked anxiously around the room for some token to hold on to. She saw the unmade bed and grabbed her mother's pillow before running out of the room.

CHAPTER 10

They drove in silence for what felt like hours even though according to the clock on the dashboard, only 20 minutes had passed. Cory watched out of her window as the neighborhoods sped by. It hadn't sunk in yet that her mother was really gone. She kept trying to tell herself it was all a horrible mistake, even though she knew she was trying to talk herself into believing a lie. She didn't want it to be real. Her mom couldn't be gone. What was she supposed to do?

Cory tried to open her eyes as wide as possible, trying to discourage tears from falling. She needed to keep her hurt to herself. She would wait to fall apart until she was alone, and then she would break. She needed time to grieve and to adjust. It frustrated her, but she didn't have that luxury. She had just been given the most devastating news of her life and now had to face being plucked from her home to live somewhere with strangers who knew nothing about her. Cory tried to bite the inside of her cheek to divert the emotional pain in her chest toward physical pain, which was much more tangible and somehow easier to deal with.

Finally, Abigail stopped the car in front of a small green house with a slightly overgrown yard and a large front window. The house looked tired. The paint was somewhat faded and the grass a little long, but overall it did look like somebody took care of it.

"Here we are." Abigail sang in a falsely optimistic tone the way adults sometimes do when they talk to small children. Cory didn't know why she bothered. It didn't help. Abigail had to know this was the worst day of her life and speaking in a happy tone would do nothing to make it better.

Cory squeezed her eyes shut as she mentally corrected herself. This wasn't the worst day of her life. It was the second worst day of her life. She had been through worse.

Abigail was out of the car and opening the trunk before Cory had enough time to swing her legs out the door.

They made their way up the sidewalk to the front stoop and rang the bell.

The house seemed so quiet, Cory began to wonder if anyone was home.

Finally, the door creaked open the width of an eye belonging to someone at least a foot shorter.

"Yeah," the owner of the eye said in a rough androgynous sounding voice.

Abigail seemed unfazed, "Ms. Grout. I am Abigail Mitchum, we spoke earlier on the phone."

"Yeah," the gravelly voice that apparently belonged to Ms. Grout repeated.

"Yes, I have Corrina Fall here for you. She will be staying with you for a short time and I thank you for your willingness to let her in your home."

Ms. Grout huffed, which led to a deep, wet-sounding cough, and then swung the door open.

Cory's eyes had to adjust to the dim light before she could take in the room.

The living room was small and bare except for an old brown recliner, a cheap television stand, and a small, old-style television.

You're Cory, huh?" She asked looking her over, eyes lingering on her duffle bag.

Cory nodded.

"Alright then, let me take you back." Ms. Grout was almost as wide as she was short. She turned and started walking down the narrow hallway without waiting to see if Cory would follow.

Cory glanced at Abigail who shrugged her shoulders and made a shooing gesture with her hands to encourage her to keep up.

There wasn't much to the house. There was a small kitchen off the living room with a round table surrounded by four white chairs. The door at the end of the hall was open revealing a small bathroom with a dusty pink shower, pink and brown tiles on the walls, and gold colored linoleum on the floor. There were also three closed doors that Cory assumed were bedrooms.

"That one there is mine. You need to stay out of that one." The woman grunted, pointing out the door on the left. "The boys stay in that one." She pointed out the door to the right of the bathroom. "Stay out of that one too."

She paused to produce another phlegmy sounding cough. Cory hoped she wasn't contagious. "This one is yours." She opened the third door to the smallest bedroom Cory had ever seen. The walls were a faded blue with nothing on them except a few stray nails and remnants of old tape. There were two twin size beds pushed against the far corners of the room, to make room for a narrow walkway between them. There was one small window between the two beds, covered with what looked like an old floral print sheet.

Cory closed her eyes longer than a blink, wishing she could go home.

"The kids are out." Ms. Grout stated. "Make yourself comfortable, but don't touch nothing. I don't want no trouble while you're here."

Cory nodded to the woman and then noticed Abigail's head peeking around her shoulder.

"Corrina, you are going to do just fine here, right?" Abigail asked.

Cory didn't know how to answer that. Of course, she wouldn't be fine. Nothing was fine in her life anymore. She was going to stay here, with strangers, and not touch anything. It didn't sound fine to her, but it wasn't like she had any choice.

Abigail took Cory's silence as an affirmation, pleased that she didn't cause any type of scene, knowing most teenagers would under the circumstances. "Good. I will keep in touch with Ms. Grout and let you know what I find about your aunt or what permanent placements we can make. I will also let her know about any funeral arrangements that are made, I am sure your aunt will be involved with that."

Abigail seemed to be checking off items in a mental list, completely oblivious to the tears that now began to flow down Cory's cheeks. Cory wiped them away as quickly as she could before turning to face the window hiding her tears.

"Alright then, I guess that's all. Ms. Grout. You have the information on Corrina and my phone number. Please call me if you need anything. Corrina, you too, you can text me if anything comes up. I will be in touch."

Cory didn't bother waving or acknowledging Abigail in any way as she left. At the moment she hated Abigail and her efficiency.

There was an old, ragged elephant on one of the beds and a nightshirt peeking out from under the pillow. Cory assumed that bed belonged to her new roommate.

She placed her duffle bag on the foot of the opposite bed and rubbed her eyes. She felt like she could either let herself break down now or she could pull out her supplies and let her mind go. Maybe when she was lost in her art, her subconscious would be able to come to terms with some of her overwhelming feelings.

She unzipped her bag, pulled out her medium

sized sketchbook and her oil pastels. She needed to think about her mother and what she looked like. The fear, sadness, and isolation faded away as Cory lost herself in the lines of her mother's jaw, the exact shade of her eyes, and the way the light played in her hair. Her mother was smiling. She was beautiful and the love for Cory shone in the eyes. She captured her mother perfectly.

"So, you're the new girl?" Cory was instantly pulled back into the cramped room of her emergency shelter. Her mental oasis shattered.

She looked at the intruder. She was a medium height with a medium build, but she carried herself in a way that let Cory know she wasn't someone to be messed with. She looked like someone who wouldn't hesitate to lash out by any means necessary to get what she wanted.

"I'm Annaliese. Who are you?" The girl barked.

Cory watched as Annaliese seemed to grow impatient waiting for an answer. Her dark eyes flashed in annoyance as she flipped her fire engine red hair over her shoulder. She looked like she was preparing herself for a fight.

Cory stared at the way the red of her hair clashed with the rich olive tones of the girl's skin. She couldn't help but think burgundy would be a much better hair color for her.

"Are you stupid? I asked your name." The girl growled menacingly, staring into her eyes looking like a dog preparing to attack. Cory was taken aback by the animosity.

Cory shook her head and wrote her name at the bottom of her mom's portrait as if she were signing her work. Then she shifted the drawing so Annaliese could read it.

The girl's eyes flicked over the drawing before

reading Cory's name. She let out a long audible breath.

"You're one of those that don't talk." She said more to herself than to Cory. She had been in foster care long enough to run across girls like Cory before. Most the time, when kids didn't talk it was better not to ask why.

Cory nodded her head. They both paused, studying each other. Annaliese's eyes were narrowed in concentration, almost as if she recognized her on some primal level. Cory wanted to break the connection by looking away, but she couldn't. She felt compelled to look at Annaliese. Her chin was a little too large and square for her face. Her nostrils slightly flared with her audible breath. Her menacing features contrasted with the delicate arch of her eyebrows, high cheekbones, and pointy elfin ears. Cory wasn't sure what to make of her.

After several minutes, Annaliese said, "You're drawing is bang-up. You do that?"

Cory exhaled a breath she didn't know she was holding. She felt relief that Annaliese had seemed to at least try not to hate her. She gave a small closed-lip smile and held up her colorfully filthy hands.

"Guess so." Annaliese laughed, her guard apparently lowered.

She started to poke through Cory's open bag sitting at the end of the bed. Cory's watched, her body stiffening at the invasion.

"Girl, you didn't bring any clothes. You just have art shit and underwear."

Cory smiled a little easier this time. She was right, she didn't really bring much other than her art supplies.

She shrugged her shoulders as a response.

"Alright then. I tell you what. I am going to help you out. I can see you need it." Annaliese said authoritatively.

A feeling of apprehension slithered through Cory's body.

Annaliese glanced to the doorway, and seeing it empty began to whisper. "Old lady is here for the money, got that. She's gonna take what she thinks she can trade or sell. You need to leave out enough that she doesn't think you're holding out, but hide the stuff you really don't want to lose."

It hadn't even occurred to Cory that someone would try to take her stuff.

Annaliese started to rifle through her bag with more of a purpose this time. She pulled half of the paintbrushes from the rubber band, took the charcoals, two sketchbooks, and the paints and set them on the bed. Then, she crawled on the floor reaching around under her own bed and pulled out a battered shoebox. She sat up on her knees, a triumphant smile on her face.

"Here you go." She said as she filled the box with Cory's supplies before sliding the sketchbooks and the box under the far corner of Cory's bed. Then she fluffed the socks, underwear, and pajamas in the duffle bag to make it look as full as it was before.

They heard footsteps and groaning coming down the hall.

Before Cory could comprehend what was happening. Her sketchbook was ripped out of her hands and swept with her color pastels under the pillow on the bed. Annaliese had effectively hidden her work just as Ms. Grout appeared in their doorway. Instinctively Cory pulled the sleeves of her sweater down over her telltale pastel smeared hands

CHAPTER 11

"**G**irls, it's time to make dinner." Ms. Grout wheezed.

"Are the guys home?" Annaliese asked.

Ms. Grout didn't seem to have heard her because she simply turned to make her way back down the hall. Cory couldn't help but wonder if she had some sort of hearing problem or if she just didn't care to talk to them.

Annaliese shrugged, unfazed. "Come one. I'll show you."

Cory followed Annaliese into the kitchen where Mrs. Grout was unlocking one of the cabinets. She was surprised to see that most of the cabinets had latches and small padlocks between the two doors. She wondered why cabinet doors in a kitchen needed to be locked in the first place. She looked at Annaliese with raised eyebrows, hoping she would get a response to her unspoken question.

She didn't.

Again, Annaliese didn't seem to notice anything usual about the situation. Perhaps, Cory thought, everything that was happening was part of the routine at the Grouts.

After three of the locks were undone, Annaliese took out and set on the counter a large pot, a box of pasta, a jar of sauce and two cans of green beans. Then she removed a strainer, a can opener, a large spoon, five plates, and five forks.

As soon as she was finished, Ms. Grout started to lock the cabinets back up. Cory watched in fascination as they moved around each other like making dinner in a minuscule kitchen with locked cabinets was a well-choreographed dance.

"Alright then. You." She pointed a fat finger toward Cory. "Set the table for four. I take my supper in the other room."

Cory nodded and began to set the small round wooden table for four as she continued to watch Annaliese out of the corner of her eye.

Annaliese didn't say anything as she turned on the stove to boil water for the pasta.

As she started to open the green beans, Cory sensed she was no longer alone in the room. She slowly turned to see two skinny boys watching her. She was surprised she didn't hear them come in. They were obviously brothers. She might have mistaken them for twins at first because they looked so much alike, but one of them was quite a bit larger. Cory guessed he was at least a year, maybe two older.

The older boy was nearly as tall as Cory, the other one about five inches shorter. She guessed maybe they were around twelve and fourteen years old. They both had dark brown eyes that sparkled with mischief, smooth clear skin, upturned noses, and small pouty lips. Their bodies were wiry, their clothes appeared to hang off their frames. Cory continued her survey and was surprised by the thick reddish, marred skin creeping out of the collar of the older boy's shirt and along the arms of the smaller boy. She tried to pull her eyes away, but she couldn't.

The boys knew she was staring, but it didn't bother them. It was who they were and they had come to terms with their burned skin a long time ago.

"Who are you?" The younger boy asked without hesitation.

Cory looked to Annaliese who thankfully took over the introductions. "Elijah, this is Cory. Cory, this is Elijah, and his brother Donovan."

Elijah smiled impishly while Donovan asked, "What's the deal, how long are you going to be here?"

"That's a rude thing to say, you are going to make her think she isn't welcomed." Annaliese teased. "Besides, she is only here until they find somewhere else for her to go."

Donovan snorted. "They always say that, don't they?"

Annaliese smiled, "yeah, I know, but I think she is really here because of a bind and they are looking for something else."

Cory shot her a questioning look. She wondered what else Annaliese knew about her situation.

"I overheard Ms. Grout talking on the phone this morning before you got here," Annaliese responded to Cory's look.

"How come you have on the Halloween makeup?" Elijah asked.

Cory couldn't help but giggle. Elijah wasn't judging her by her looks, he was honestly asking. It was refreshing to be asked instead of slyly stared out by people who were pretending not to notice her and her mask.

"Eli, leave her alone." She turned to Cory, "don't mind him, Cory. He's just curious and obvious lacks a brain to mouth filter."

Cory shrugged her shoulders.

"What's the deal, don't you talk?" Elijah asked.

Cory shook her head no.

"Oh."

There was a brief uncomfortable silence before Elijah added, "that's okay. Lots of kids don't talk. Hey Donovan, you remember that one kid, that one kid that didn't talk. What was his name?"

Donovan shrugged his shoulders.

"Yeah, I don't remember his name either." Elijah

continued, "but he didn't talk either, then one day he did." He started to stir the boiling noodles on the stove, apparently finished telling his story.

Annaliese finished cooking the dinner and getting everything ready. She brought Ms. Grout a plate and set it on her TV stand in the other room.

Cory, Annaliese, and the boys sat around the table to eat theirs. Cory couldn't help but think it was nice to be surrounded by people her own age.

Before she got her first bite chewed and swallowed, Cory realized the others were scraping their plates. They had eaten so fast, they were done.

"Sorry, Cory, but the last one done cleans up. Just wash and dry everything and then let Ms. Grout know so she can lock everything back up, okay? When you're done, come back to the room. We have to keep quiet and lights go out at 10, got it?"

Cory nodded while Annaliese and the boys were instantly gone.

Her new home was definitely going to take some getting used to.

The next morning at breakfast, the kids scrambled to take a package of pop tarts and get out the door, hoping to make the bus on time.

Cory was at a total loss. Was she supposed to go to school? How did she get there? She didn't even know where exactly she was, much less where the school was.

She waited in hope Ms. Grout would say something, but she didn't.

Cory cleaned up the kitchen and slowly got dressed in her room.

She tore out a strip of paper from one of her sketchbooks and wrote "school?"

She took the note to Ms. Grout.

"What? You're not going to school. You are not enrolled in school anymore."

Cory gave her a perplexed look.

"I can't get you to your old school and they don't know what to do with you just yet. You need to give your case manager some time and then they'll figure it out. For now, no school. I do need you to do a few chores around here, though. Everyone has to pull their weight."

Cory spent the morning working through her list of chores, hoping Abigail Mitchum would call with an update, but nothing happened.

After lunch, she went to her room and closed the door. She pulled out two pieces of charcoal from the box under her bed. Instinctively she felt that it would be better if her paints stayed hidden.

She positioned herself comfortably on her bed, ready to draw in her book. She noticed her duffle bag and saw that it was unzipped. Cory was certain she had zipped it closed that morning when she got dressed. There must be some truth to Annaliese's warnings about Ms. Grout going through her things.

She felt a shot of anger pulse through her. She was angry about the invasion of privacy and the fact it was done when Cory was working through a list of household chores.

She shook her head, trying to rid herself of the feeling. It wasn't worth it. She wouldn't be here long and there would be something new.

A little voice in Cory's mind asked if a new situation would be any better. Maybe this was as good as things were going to get for her. She would always be living among strangers. Strangers who didn't care what happened to her or respect her privacy.

She started to draw the streets of an empty city. There were no cars or people. The buildings hulked over the horizon but were void of life. She drew herself in the distance, standing in the street. Alone. Her chest tightened. She hated feeling so isolated and unable to speak for herself.

Cory hoped Abigail would call to give her an update. She wanted to know what was happening with her mother's funeral and what would be happening to her. It bothered her that the adults in her life, who didn't know her at all, were planning what was best for her. She wondered if it would always be like this for her. For the first time in years, she wanted to be able to use her voice.

CHAPTER 12

She was so lost in her work, she barely noticed when Annaliese and the boys came home from school.

The three of them crashed into the room to see what Cory was up to. They were shocked by her drawing. Annaliese asked if she could hang it in their room.

Cory shrugged, ripped the paper out of the book, and then rummaged in her duffle bag to pull out some hairspray. She pumped a few squirts over the drawing to set the charcoal and handed it to Annaliese who reverently set it on her bed and went to look for some tape or tacks.

Elijah smiled a toothy smile at her and asked if he could draw with her.

Cory nodded as he scampered away to his room, probably, she thought, to gather his supplies.

He was back in minutes with, as she suspected, a sketchbook, a pencil, and an old box of crayons.

He scooched himself beside her on the bed.

Cory did a double take as she noticed he wasn't holding just any sketchbook. He was holding her sketchbook.

She yanked at the corner of the book and opened her eyes wide at Elijah, silently demanding an answer.

Elijah chuckled, "oh, yeah, I can't believe I forgot. I borrowed this from you last night after dinner. I would have asked, but you were doing dishes and I didn't want to interrupt." He gave her an angelic look.

Cory was shocked. There had been a few thefts at the art room of her school in the past. A couple times it turned out not to be theft, but people misplacing their things. She always put her things away in her designated area before, and nobody ever touched them. At home, her mother never invaded her privacy. It just wasn't done. She couldn't believe Elijah snuck into her room, then went through her things and helped himself.

She grabbed the book out of his hands and pointed to the door.

"Aww come on, Cor. I didn't mean anything by it. I was going to give it back." He whined.

Cory gave him a death glare and pointed again at the door again.

"Okay, fine, geesh, you don't have to be so dramatic." He grumbled as he left the room.

Annaliese, who had returned with a roll of masking tape around her wrist giggled. "He's always doing that Cory. So is Donovan. They are a pair of sticky fingers, those two. You always have to keep your eyes open for them but don't worry, they'll give your stuff back if you ask for it."

Cory furled her eyebrows while her lips turned into a grimace. She shook her head. She couldn't believe the audacity.

"What do you want to do, now?" She asked. "We have a couple of hours before dinner."

Cory shrugged her shoulders and held up her sketchbook.

"Yeah, okay. You can draw. Maybe I'll get my homework done for once."

Cory watched Annaliese move. She was so sure and confident yet, feminine and graceful in her movements. She had a spirit of independence in everything she did. Cory admired it. She felt compelled to draw her, to capture what she was seeing.

She lay on the floor and reached under the bed until she found the box with her supplies. She gathered the box of oil pastels and her slightly larger sketchbook and set to work.

Annaliese dozed off before Cory was finished. Cory kept working. She took the liberty of changing her hair color from fire-engine red to deep burgundy, the color she thought it should be. The result was stunning. In her drawing, Annaliese looked confident and raw, yet beautiful and calm. She had the strength Cory wanted to see in herself, but was never able to capture in her portraits. Was it because she wasn't strong or because she didn't think she was?

Cory finished her work and hid her supplies under the bed. She stretched out and thought about the options the Abigail explained to her in the car yesterday. At the time, Cory heard the words, but couldn't quite comprehend them. Now, that she had a little distance, she could think them over in depth.

Abigail told her she would be looking for a placement that would keep her until she turned eighteen. Hopefully a family member, maybe her aunt would step up, or possibly a group home situation. Abigail had said that she hoped her placement could be permanent for her, but there were no guarantees. At the age of eighteen, she would be out of the foster system even though she would be going to school until she turned twenty-one. Most group homes weren't set up to house adults with adolescents. The social worker mentioned living with a foster family was a remote possibility, unlikely because she was an older teen who had special needs. Most families wouldn't want to take a chance on her, she'd be considered dangerous.

Cory grunted in disgust as she thought about herself being dangerous, she was the farthest thing from it. She didn't do anything besides art. She never went anywhere, never got into trouble, and kept completely to herself. Although, she supposed to most people the sight of her was a little scary. Her hair, her clothes, her makeup looked like she could be trouble. Plus, not talking tended to make people around her uneasy.

She wasn't sure what to hope for. The idea of a group home never bothered her before, but now that she had a small taste of what it would be like, she didn't want it to be her future.

She felt so lost and more alone than she ever had before.

Would a faceless caseworker always make her decisions, moving her around from place to place as she aged or as situations changed? Would she always be watching her things; afraid they would be stolen? Would there be worse things that happened to her in random group homes for the rest of her life?

She was sixteen and wished more than anything that she could live on her own, but that wasn't one of the possible options. It would never be an option for her. She would grow up to be an adult, a barely functioning adult who can't even speak. Certainly, she would never be able to make decisions for herself.

She slipped out of her room and into the bathroom. With the shower running, she sat on the toilet and let herself cry. She cried for herself, her future, and her mother. She cried until her throat was raw and her eyes, nearly swollen from tears.

CHAPTER 13

It was Wednesday afternoon before Abigail finally called with an update.

Cory was settled on her bed, sketchbook on her lap when she heard the phone ring. It was only her third full day, but she had fallen into a routine. In the morning, she got up and ate breakfast with Annaliese and the boys. Then she'd start on her chore list for Ms. Grout. It had taken her until lunchtime each day to finish. After lunch, she would draw until everyone came home. She'd draw for a while before dinner and again before bed. She had yet to get her paints out. She didn't want to attract attention to her paints and risk them getting stolen by Ms. Grout, or borrowed indefinitely without permission by Elijah, even though she suspected Elijah had already seen them in her hiding place and made the decision not to take them.

She listened as Ms. Grout wheezed hello into the phone.

"Yeah." She said to the caller. "Yeah, she's here, let me go get her."

There was a long pause. Cory crept silently into the living room.

"What do you mean she can't talk on the phone? She's just in the other room."

Another pause.

"What do you mean she doesn't talk. She's been living here."

Cory froze. She was surprised Ms. Grout had only just realized she hadn't spoken a word since her arrival and the only reason she found out was because someone told her. For some reason, Cory felt like she had been rejected. She had spent half her life trying to hide her true self, apparently, she had done such a good job, someone who was supposedly caring for her didn't even realize that she hadn't spoken while living under her roof. Did she want to go through life without anyone knowing the real her? She could imagine her life stretched out before her and it seemed destined to be impossibly lonely now that her mother was gone.

She blinked away the tears forming in her eyes and promised herself to think about it later. For now, she wanted to know what Abigail had to say.

Ms. Grout hung up the phone and appeared to look closely at Cory in what might have been the first time since her arrival.

"That was your caseworker," she finally said. "She is going to be picking you up in an hour. They found your aunt. You will be staying with her. They are going to have your mom's funeral next Monday." The effort of speaking must have rattled something loose in Ms. Grout's lungs because when she finished telling Cory the plan, she began to deeply hack into a tissue.

Hiding her grimace at the sounds coming from her caregiver, Cory nodded and turned to go back to her room. She didn't need to be told it was time to pack up her belongings. Even though she hadn't been there long, it took her awhile to make sure she had everything.

She expected Abigail to arrive well before Annaliese and the boys got home from school. It made her feel a little melancholy as she suspected Abigail wouldn't want to wait around for them to get home so she could say goodbye, not like she'd use words anyway.

She tore the portrait of Annaliese out of her sketchbook and set it on top of her bed.

She paused for a moment before taking her small sketchbook and a drawing pencil out of her bag. She quietly walked to the boys' room to slide them under Elijah's pillow. It took her a minute to think of a memento for Donovan. He wasn't into art, but he had admired her bracelet. She pulled the black braided leather cord off her wrist and left it on his dresser. She was amazed how quickly her time had come and gone. She would miss the three of them.

Her duffle bag was packed and ready on the foot of her bed. Cory didn't want to wait in the front room with Ms. Grout. Uncharacteristically, she didn't even want to draw. What she did was lay on her bed and think about what the next move would be like. She would be living with an aunt she hadn't seen in years. An aunt who had gotten into such a horrendous fight with her mother, they had stopped all communication.

Two years, Cory thought, in just two years, less than two years really, she would be eighteen and legally able to move out. She was pretty sure she could endure anything for two years.

She tried to ignore the fact that when she turned eighteen she would probably end up in a group home, much like the one she was leaving today. She'd have a lifetime of living in a group home with people going through her things, telling her what to do, and not letting her be herself.

Maybe, she thought, it was time to revise her plan. Maybe she didn't want the life that had been laid out for her at school in monthly planning meetings. Maybe right now she really didn't have a say in what happened to her. But in two years, she would be eighteen and she needed different options. Maybe she could have a say in what happened to her.

Maybe the gorilla at the zoo could use a painting buddy?

CHAPTER 14

A knock at the door caused Cory's eyes to fly open as she sat bolt upright. She was surprised that she had fallen asleep while she had been waiting for Abigail's arrival. A quick look at the clock told her it would be at least forty-five minutes before Annaliese and the boys would get home from school. She wished she had a chance for a goodbye. She would miss them.

She stood and straightened her rumpled black clothes as best she could. She pulled the cover tight on the bed, picked up her mother's pillow, and swung her duffle over her shoulder. She left the room without a backward glance, determined she would be strong for whatever was in store for her.

Abigail looked the same as she always did as she stood just inside Ms. Grout's door. She wore a brown tweed skirt and a burgundy colored top. Seeing her should have been reassuring, instead, it made Cory's heart race as a layer of sweat broke out across her skin. Abigail said goodbye, Ms. Grout grunted her response, and then Abigail led Cory to her car.

On the way to her aunt's house, Cory's mind was spinning. She missed her mom desperately and felt so lost over her living situation. Her life had been disintegrated in an instant and she had no idea how to go about coming up with something new. The ambiguity was wearing at her. She knew she would be able to withstand almost anything for a while, but she needed to know what she was facing in order to prepare for it. Not knowing what was coming next was driving her crazy.

Abigail tried to make conversation. She told Cory that her aunt was happy to have her live with her. Cory didn't acknowledge Abigail but was glad to hear about her aunt. She remembered her aunt as having a bright personality and was quick to laugh and generous with hugs. Her memories had good feelings tied to them. She had a hard time reconciling those memories with the fact that her aunt had dropped out of her life. She remembered her mother and her aunt having a huge fight over something. She remembered they had screamed at each other. Cory had never known what the fight was about, but the fallout from it was severe.

She never saw her aunt again and her mother never mentioned her. Cory had written questions asking about her aunt, but her mom never answered and eventually, she let it go.

Cory didn't know why, after what had happened, her aunt would ever agree to take her in. Even if it would only be for two years. She wondered if the rift was so great her aunt would take out her residual anger on her. Cory shuddered to think about it and hoped living with her aunt was the right option for her. She wished she had a choice, but didn't think her life would be any better in foster care.

She knew a little about foster care. There were a lot of kids at her school who were in the system. Because each of her classmates had some sort of special needs, they usually stayed in their placements for longer periods of time. Foster parents who took in special needs kids usually had some sort of training to take care of them and she heard teachers talk every once in a while, about how they got paid a little more a month to care for special kids. Maybe if things didn't work out with her aunt, a foster family would take her in, but the idea of living with strangers was becoming less and less appealing. It had worked okay with Ms. Grout, but there were some challenges and would she be as lucky next time?

Maybe a group home would be the best option. She could live with others who were like her. Being supervised all the time wouldn't be too bad, at least she could get away during the day when she was at school.

Cory was yanked from her thoughts when the car stopped outside of a well-kept, brick covered duplex. It had matching white trimmed front doors on opposite sides of a flower covered front porch.

She was surprised that she remembered this house even though it had been years since she thought about it. She remembered running around the yard, playing with other kids in the neighborhood. She remembered her mom dropping her off there when she needed a babysitter. She remembered watching movies in the living room with a dark-haired girl, slightly older than she was.

She hadn't expected the flood of memories. She hadn't remembered any of it until she saw the house.

Before they got out of the car, a tall slender woman with shoulder-length curly blond hair and piercing teal colored eyes opened the front door on the right and started walking toward them. She looked so much like her mother, Cory wanted to rush to hug her. As she watched, she noticed the way the woman carried herself was completely different from her mom. This woman had a lightness and self-assurance in the way she walked. Her mother's movements were always somehow guarded.

Cory let out a breath that she didn't realize she had been holding.

"Corrina," the woman, her Aunt Miranda, breathed before launching herself onto Cory's arms, pulling her into a giant bear hug.

Cory felt her warm embrace. It felt so comforting and loving. She remembered this version of Aunt Miranda, she was someone that she loved and trusted when she was little. The odd thing was that in her memories, her aunt had never called her Corinna. Her aunt called her Cory. She felt so conflicted as she tried to wrap her mind around the falling out this woman had had with her mother. She wished she knew more about what had happened between them. She didn't want to disrespect her mom by liking Miranda.

"Let me look at you sweetheart," Miranda said as she pushed against Cory's shoulders, causing an arm's length distance between them. Miranda's eyes seemed to want to take in every detail of Cory's appearance. Cory could only sense love, not judgment or anger, directed towards her.

Miranda gently ran her hand down Cory's black locks. She looked past her heavily made-up face into her eyes before taking in her layers of concealing black clothes.

"Corrina, you have changed so much." Her words expressed a whispered awe, "and yet you are still the same. I am so happy to see you." Her eyes clouded over before she added, "I just wish.... I wish it could have been under different circumstances, but at least you are here now."

She leaned in to kiss her cheek. "How are you doing?" The look in Miranda's eyes burned with sincerity. Cory wanted to look away and stay strong, but she couldn't. Her nose started to run while tears dripped from her eyes. She hated the way her tears were always so close to the edge. All it took was a single question and they'd start to fall.

She nodded as she ran her fingers along the bottom of her eyes. She had to pull it together. She had to stay in control.

Miranda seemed to understand. She nodded and pulled Cory into another smothering hug, before acknowledging Abigail and thanking her for all that she had done.

The three of them walked into the tiny house. Miranda gave them a quick tour.

Cory's room was small but larger than the one she'd shared with Annaliese at Ms. Grout's place. It had a single bed with a new looking purple comforter and a small white nightstand with an old-fashioned lamp next to it. There was a small closet and a dresser built into the wall next to the door.

The room looked clean and comfortable.

"I hope you like it here. We can change anything you want." Miranda stammered. "I thought about getting a desk for you in here when I found out you would be coming, but then I wondered if you'd rather use the space for an easel or maybe a drafting table. We could maybe add a bookshelf for your supplies. I thought we would figure it out after you got situated."

Cory flinched as she mentioned her artwork, how had she known she would prefer an easel over a desk? Her eyes flew to Mirandas in a silent demand for answers.

Miranda seemed to sense Cory's question because she added "I saw some of your work at the mall. There was a display showcasing work from students at your school. It was very good. I was impressed. I figured you would want space to paint or draw here."

Cory gaped. She searched her mind for the dim memory of her principal telling her about the exhibit at the mall. It seemed too long ago, yet her aunt had seen it and had known that her work was in it.

She thought about how long it had taken them to get to this house. It hadn't been that long of a drive. It dawned on her that she had grown up living in close proximity to her aunt.

She had lived close to family, yet she had always

felt isolated. She had always felt like she and her mother had no one, but that wasn't true. There had been a huge fight between her aunt and her mother, but did they have to let it ruin their relationship? Couldn't they have gotten over it, no matter what it was about?

Cory's head pounded as she tried to reconcile her memories of her aunt with the love she felt for her mother and her feelings of growing up isolated. Could things have been different? What would her life have been like if her aunt and mother hadn't had a fight? Would things be different for her today?

CHAPTER 15

That evening, Cory and Miranda danced around each other trying not to invade each other's personal space. Cory was trying to be an easy guest. Miranda was trying to be welcoming. The result was awkward and uncomfortable.

By the time dinner was over and the kitchen clean, Cory wanted nothing more than to hide in her room, drawing before bed.

Thankfully, Miranda left her alone. She stayed up late painting and was surprised that Miranda let her sleep in the next morning. It was close to eleven before Cory's need to pee pulled her from her covers.

She glanced at her painting from the night before. It was a fantasy-scape, a type of brooding fairy dwelling that at first seemed whimsical, but on closer inspection, was somewhat menacing. The colors swirled together in a dreamlike pattern offering sweetness before the beginning of the nightmare.

Instead of getting sidetracked reworking her painting, she got dressed and made her way to the kitchen. She didn't know what to expect but was hoping she'd be able to scrounge some food without incident.

She was surprised to see Miranda with her laptop open at the kitchen table. There were papers spread around her held in place by what appeared to be a half-full cup of coffee. Miranda's hair was pulled into a haphazard ponytail at the back of her head. She had dark rimmed glasses perched on the bridge of her nose. Cory hadn't seen them yesterday and suspected they were reading glasses needed for her aunt's work on the computer. Miranda appeared to be working diligently while wearing a purple faded t-shirt and a pair of baggy gray sweatpants.

She smiled when she looked up and saw Cory entering the kitchen. "Hey there, sleeping beauty. Do you always sleep in this late?"

Cory shrugged her shoulders and made no move to further enter the room.

"Come on let's get you some," her voice trailed away as she looked at her watch, "well, I suppose you could have either breakfast or lunch at this time of day. Let's take a look at your options and you can figure what you want. Okay?"

She proceeded to show Cory a plethora of easily prepared food in the pantry, refrigerator, and freezer. Miranda was trying so hard to be accommodating. While Cory appreciated her efforts, she was having trouble reconciling the fact that there had been a reason they hadn't seen each other for years. Cory wondered if her aunt was really the kind smiling woman she seemed to be, or if there was something below the surface waiting to spring until her guard was down. Something that had caused the fallout with her mother. Cory felt certain there had to be something off about Miranda because why else would her mother not talk to her sister for years, a sister who lived in the same town?

Miranda chattered to Cory about her work as a wedding planner while she slowly ate a slice of peanut butter and banana toast across from her at the kitchen table.

After describing her dealings with caterers, diva-like brides, and crazy photographers, she proceeded to fill Cory in about Mr. Bradley next door. He was an eighty-five-year-old man whose mind was as sharp as a tack and had a wicked sense of humor, but whose body was rapidly deteriorating. Cory was looking forward to meeting him.

Then her aunt went on to describe details about the neighborhood, where to shop, what kids to look for and which ones to avoid. Cory shuddered. She would avoid all of them, she didn't hang out with kids her age. She stayed in her room to paint.

Her aunt went on to spend a lot of time describing the school and what kids in the neighborhood did for fun. Idly, Cory wondered when she would be going back to school. But at the moment she felt so exhausted, she didn't want to make her aunt remember that she needed to go any sooner than she had to.

Finally, Miranda started to explain the funeral arrangements. It was going to be on Monday afternoon. Her mom had been cremated. That word caused a heavy weight of finality to settle over her. There was no way she could delude herself any further that her mother would be coming back, not that she really believed it, but it was something to hang on to for a little while. Cory bit the inside of her cheek to help hold back her tears. She nodded as Miranda continued to fill her in on the details. She wondered why Miranda would go to so much trouble for the two of them and maybe a few friends to pay their last respects. They could have simply taken the urn and said kind words about her mother in a park or something.

CHAPTER 16

After her discussion with Miranda, Cory was physically and mentally drained. She excused herself with a nod and a half smile and went to her room where she fell on top of her bedspread and closed her eyes. Miranda seemed so much like her mother. She had the feeling Miranda was taking her in because she genuinely loved her and not because she felt obligated.

Lost in thought Cory wondered once again what had caused the rift between Miranda and her mom. They seemed so alike. What could have happened that drove them so completely apart?

Miranda's soft knock at the door pulled Cory from her musings.

"Corrina," she said, poking her head in the door. "Did you want to go with me to the school?"

Cory felt the confused expression on her face.

"We need to get you registered," Miranda explained.

Cory still felt confused.

"We need to get you registered for school. Your new school. It isn't far. I thought you might want to go with me to check it out. You won't officially start until after the... until next week some time. I thought you might want to come with me to get the registration papers so you can get a feel for it. It might help you ease into it."

Cory's confusion melted into horror as Miranda's words sunk in. She couldn't go to a new school. Everything would be different. She started with a small shake of her head that became bigger. She squeezed her eyes shut in an attempt to erase Miranda's existence. She could not go to a new school. She had her life mapped out at her old school, not that she had exciting prospects, but it was what she knew. More than anything, she wanted to scream the word NO at her aunt.

Breathing hard, she felt like she was drowning. The word was there on the tip of her tongue. She wanted to say or scream or cry the word no. It was one syllable. She could say that one small word. She wanted to; she was so close.

Instead, she continued to squeeze her eyes shut and violently shook her head.

She heard Miranda take steps into her room and felt the bed dip as she sat next to her.

"Corrina, don't be like that. You know you have to go to school. I can't get you to your old one every day, and besides. I think you need more... You don't talk, that is your choice, but you need to be challenged and not allowed to simply exist."

Cory pushed her fingers into her ears so she wouldn't have to listen to Miranda's use of her full name or her explanations. She knew she was being childish, but thinking of switching schools felt like she would lose the last shred of normalcy in her life. People there were used to her and her oddities. If she moved, she'd be nothing more than the freaky girl who didn't talk. Everything else had been taken away from her, school was the last thing she could count on.

Miranda tried to talk with her over the next two days, but whenever she did, Cory would close her eyes as tight as she could and jam her fingers in her ears. When Miranda wasn't around, Cory sketched in her large sketchbook. She drew angry pictures of herself falling off cliffs or drowning in black water. They didn't take away her fearful, angry, or aggressive feelings, but they did help her feel like they could be managed.

On the third day, Miranda stomped into her room, apparently done trying to reason. "Damn it, Corrina. Don't you see what is going on?" Her eyes flashed with frustration.

Cory didn't know what Miranda meant and she didn't care. She just pulled herself tighter into a ball on her bed, stuck her finger in her ear, and closed her eyes.

"No, you don't." Miranda pulled Cory's hands away and declared, "I am not letting you give up. This is exactly what you have done all your life. She allowed you do it and it isn't right. She coddled you and didn't let you mature into your potential."

Cory's eyes flashed open meeting Miranda's eyes with silent confrontation.

"I know you went through hell, Corrina. I know it was hell on your mom. It was unimaginable for everyone who ever knew either one of you. What you went through, no child... no, no person should ever have had to go through that."

Miranda took a deep breath to steady her resolve. She had to say what was burning at her. She had to speak her mind to get Cory to understand. She was going to be an adult soon and she couldn't let her past rob her of a future.

"Your mom felt intensely guilty for what happened to you. She couldn't help but feel that if she had never left your father, he wouldn't have lost his mind. He wouldn't have done what he did if it wasn't for her."

Cory violently shook her head back and forth at Miranda's words. It wasn't her mother's fault. It was her father's. Nothing was her mother's fault. Her mother loved her and took care of her. She was the only person who ever did, the only person who ever would.

Cory wanted to shrivel up into a ball, not to die.

Dying seemed like too much to hope for. She simply wanted to cease to exist. She wanted to disappear without a trace, leaving no memory behind that she had ever been.

Miranda softly sat at the edge of the bed and rested her arm on top of Cory's waist. She spoke quietly "Corrina, I have always loved you and I have always loved your mother. She wanted everything for you. When everything happened with your father. It broke her, just as he intended. That night they told her you died. I thought she would lose her mind from grief. Then they told her it was a mistake, that you were alive and were being rushed to the hospital." Miranda stopped talking and seemed to Cory to be lost in thought for several minutes.

"Then, at the hospital, they told her to prepare for your death, but then you didn't die. Then they told her it didn't look good. They worked on you for hours before they got you stabilized. They told her to prepare for you to be significantly brain damaged. She wanted more than anything for it to have been her and not you at the house that day." Miranda's voice trailed off again as she seemed to fight with the memories of the horror her sister and niece had been through.

"But you surprised everyone." Miranda gently stroked the hair at Cory's temple. "You survived, but your mother couldn't reconcile her guilt with your survival. She felt the overwhelming need to protect you from everything. She didn't want you to hurt ever again. When you didn't talk, she didn't try to make you. She tried to keep you from it. She took over by doing everything for you. She was trying to love you, but her love was too much, too overpowering. You became completely dependent on her while the real you began to fade away."

Cory's breath hitched as she stifled a sob. Her nose

was running, and she felt the tears welling up in her eyes.

"She showed her love in the wrong way, Corrina. It's what we fought about. I hated the way she didn't let you do anything in order to keep you from getting hurt. Her heart was always in the right place. Everything she did was out of love, but it was wrong." Miranda gave her a look that oozed sincerity. Cory wanted to believe her, but she felt so overwhelmed she didn't know what to think.

Miranda slid off the bed in order to squat down and put her face at Cory's eye level. "Corrina, she loved you to the point of hurting you. Maybe she hurt you more than he did. He tried to kill your body, but she loved you so much, she took away your spirit. She kept you from being able to function in the world. You have been so isolated and kept from doing anything. I love you enough to want more for you."

Cory felt frozen. She couldn't move. She couldn't breathe.

"In order for you to have a life of your own, we are going to enroll you into a normal school where you will learn to be a normal kid with the future you design. I want that for you." She swallowed and said nothing more for a long moment before she finally continued. " You were never a kid who should have gone to that school. Yes, you needed time to recover, but then you needed help to get back out there, to prove he didn't take everything from you."

"She couldn't give that to you, Corrina. She loved you so much and she was sure you were going to die. It broke her. When you survived, she changed. She felt like she had to protect you from everything. She lived her life trying to keep you from living yours. She did it to keep you safe. She needed to keep you safe above all else, even if that meant keeping you from actually living." Miranda's words were rushed as she forced them out of her mouth.

"You can't let your past steal your future. I want to show you that you can be an independent person who makes their own decisions and has a life. You can do beautiful things, and not just through your art. You can have it all. We don't need to go to the school tomorrow but after the funeral. Would you try?" She finished in a quiet whisper.

Cory wanted to be angry. She stared into her aunt's face. She could see nothing but compassion and love in her eyes. She wondered if her aunt could see the self-doubt and reluctance in her own.

Was this really the reason her mom fought with Miranda all those years ago? Was Miranda right that her mother tried to protect her to the point of extreme isolation? She felt incompetent in everything except art? Could she be more? Could she be independent someday? Would a normal school be the way get there? It was worth a try, wasn't it?

She gave Miranda a small, uncertain nod.

"Oh Corrina, I am so proud of you, honey." Her aunt grabbed her and pulled her into a fierce hug. Cory closed her eyes, pretending for a moment, it was her mother pulling her close. She wanted to love and be loved by Miranda, but Miranda didn't even know her name. Not her real name anyway. She wondered how they could have a real relationship if Miranda didn't even know her name. Unfortunately, she couldn't just tell her. Telling her was what a normal person would do. Cory wasn't normal. She couldn't tell her, but she could show her. Couldn't she?

Miranda gave Cory a kiss on the top of her head and sniffling, she left the room.

Cory sat for a moment and then pulled out a set of blue and black Sharpie markers. She looked in the mirror and then carefully drew a perfect black rectangle at an angle across her forehead. At the top of the rectangle, she wrote "Hello, my name is..." in letters so neat they could have been typed. She picked up the blue marker and in the middle of the rectangle, she wrote CORY in large, childlike block letters. Pleased with her new, semi-permanent nametag, she left her room to find her aunt.

She found Miranda in the kitchen making tea.

"Corrina, honey," her voice trailed off as she glanced over and read Cory's nametag.

"Cory?" She asked.

Cory nodded.

"Oh, Cory, I am so sorry. I should have known. You were always Cory. I just thought you went by Corrina now that you were grown up. I'm sorry honey."

Tears threatened in her eyes. Cory liked when her aunt used her name. She felt more like family and less like a stranger.

Miranda leaned in to examine Cory's handiwork. "Is that going to come off, sweetie?

Cory's smile slowly spread across her face before she bit her bottom lip and shrugged her shoulders.

"You know you could have just written me a note on a piece of paper, right?" Miranda laughed and pulled her closer to kiss her hair. Cory felt her cheeks flush as she considered what she had done. Yes, a note would have worked. Why hadn't she thought of that? She bit her lip and told herself she would have to work harder to try to think more like a normal person. Clearly, it wasn't natural for her to think like everyone else.

On Sunday, Miranda took Cory back to her mother's house. The plan was for Cory to pack what she wanted with her, start to organize what could be donated, and figure out what she wanted in storage for when she got her own place.

It felt surreal for Cory to be thinking about having her own place. She had never considered it a possibility before, she was still unsure, but maybe it could happen. She didn't bother trying to tell Miranda about her group home plans. Maybe she could hope for more someday. Maybe she'd be able to be independent. She really liked the thought, more than she could have imagined.

While they cleaned, cried, packed, and organized, Cory could see that her mother and Miranda were alike in many ways. She was thoughtful and kind. She talked to Cory but didn't expect her to respond. She didn't insist on making her talk. She felt a growing connection between herself and Miranda. She was glad she was a part of her life again.

When she was on a stepladder pulling boxes off the top of her mother's closet, Cory found a set of journals. They were dusty and pushed into the far back corner. It surprised her that she had never seen them before, although she would have missed them today if she hadn't been on the ladder.

She climbed off the stool to page through the journals. Her fingers traced the familiar handwriting. They had been her mother's. She couldn't believe she found her mother's diaries. She wanted to read them to feel close to her mother. She noticed one of the books was completely filled in while the second only had a few pages written on. Her stomach clenched uncomfortably, even though her mother was gone, she felt like reading them would be an invasion of privacy. She wasn't sure what to do. She needed to think about it later. Carefully, she took the journals and slid them under her clothes in one of the boxes she planned to take to Miranda's. Even if she never read them. She wanted to have them with her forever.

CHAPTER 17

Monday morning, the sun streamed through her window revealing a beautifully bright, cloudless day. She couldn't help but feel that even the weather was conspiring against her. She wanted darkness and rain, something that matched her mood and better matched a funeral. What was it about her that made her such a misfit with everyone and everything around her?

She dressed mechanically in a sleeveless, long black, crushed velvet dress that buttoned down the front from her collarbone to just above the floor. She pulled on her black combat boots and added a few black and silver bracelets to each wrist.

She sat on the side of her bed with a brush, systematically smoothing through the snarls. It was slow and painful to work through her neglected hair, but the process gave her something to focus on besides the fact she was going to her mother's funeral in just a few hours. She held her hair by the ends, working a few inches straight, before taking on a few more inches closer to her head.

She examined her reflection when she was finished. Her hair was thick, black, and shiny. It was desperately in need of a trim. She couldn't remember the last time she had gotten it cut. She was tempted to pick up a pair of scissors and do it herself, but restrained herself. Instead, she plaited it into a long braid down her back.

She didn't have the energy to fully apply her makeup. She kept it light, light for her anyway. It made her look younger, softer somehow. Her improvised nametag was only faintly visible. Most people wouldn't notice it unless they really looked at her. She was pleased that her eyes didn't look as puffy and bloodshot as she expected they would today after a weekend of crying.

She was ready to go. There was nothing more for her to do except wait until her aunt told her it was time to go. She picked up a black ballpoint pen and started to draw a tribal design on the inside of her pale left forearm.

Eventually, a knock at the door pulled her back to the present. She wasn't sure where her mind had gone. She only knew she hadn't felt the passage of time as she pulled the pen across her tender flesh, wrist to elbow, over and over again. Her only indication that it had been awhile was the intricate design that now covered most of her forearm.

"Cory, are you ready?" Her aunt said without commenting on her ink adornments.

She nodded and stood to follow her aunt out the door. Miranda looked somber and sophisticated. Her eyes were slightly puffy and her nose red, telltale signs that she had been crying. This pleased and surprised Cory. Maybe she wasn't the only one who loved and would miss her mother. Even though she knew Miranda's love for her mom would never be equal to her own, she wouldn't be completely alone in her grief. She felt comforted.

They drove in silence to a church not far from the house. Cory had been surprised last week when Miranda told her the funeral would be held in a church. Cory's mother didn't practice organized religion and they had never gone to a service. It hadn't bothered her before that Miranda had chosen a church for the service, but now that it was about to start, she didn't know what she was supposed to do. She worried she would make a mistake.

As she got out of the car, she tried to soothe herself with the knowledge that it was only her and her aunt. Her aunt wouldn't mind if she messed something up.

The church was large and empty except for a few souls dressed in black, kneeling in pews possibly lost in prayer.

Cory had never seen them before.

She stuck close to her aunt's side as they made their way to the front row nearest the small table that held her mother's silver urn next to her portrait she drew only days before at Ms. Grouts. Miranda had it framed in a clear crystal frame.

Cory closed her eyes, the tears instantly rolling down her cheeks. She was kicking herself for not remembering to bring something to wipe her eyes and nose.

Miranda opened her purse and handed Cory a new pocket pack of tissues. Gratefully, Cory nodded her thanks.

Together they sat silently crying waiting for the service to begin. Somewhere in her subconscious mind Cory heard shuffling and noises as the church began to fill, but the meaning of those noises did not register to her.

Finally, the minister stepped onto the alter beginning the service. His eyes focused on Cory and Miranda for a moment before pursuing the rest of the attendees. Cory followed his gaze by glancing over her shoulder.

Her breath caught as she took in the nearly full church. She was shocked. Why were there so many people? She was pretty sure her mother didn't even know that many people, much less have them care enough to show up at her funeral.

She looked questioningly at Miranda, convinced there was some sort of mistake. They weren't in the wrong place. Cory knew that because her mother's urn and picture were at the front of the church. Could all of these other people have come to the wrong service by accident? There were so many of them. Miranda gave no indication acknowledging Cory's confusion, she was listening intently to the minister's words while she dabbed at her at her nose with her tissue.

Cory faced forward and tried her best to focus. Between thoughts of her mother and the knowledge that so many had come to her funeral made it nearly impossible understand the minister's words.

When it was over, Cory and Miranda stood at the front of the church near her mother's ashes.

Person after person came up to them, hugging Cory and kissing her on the cheek. No one seemed to notice that Cory didn't speak, but they did seem to know who she was. They offered compassionate words as if they had known her mother well. Maybe they did, but how? When?

Cory felt a sense of overwhelming confusion. Who were all these people?

Before the church completely emptied, a young woman, probably a few years older than herself walked up to them. She would be considered tall to most people, but she was a couple inches shorter than Cory. She had naturally black, glossy hair cut into a smooth bob. Her skin was the rich color of espresso. She was beautiful, but the thing that stuck out most prominently to Cory and probably everyone else who had ever seen her was her beautiful teal eyes fringed in long black eyelashes.

Because of her dark coloring, her teal eyes were especially striking. They were impossible to look away from. The strangest thing about them was they were the exact shade of her own, and Miranda's, and her mother's. As Cory thought about it, she was fairly certain there had been others here today with the same eye color. She was irritated with herself that she hadn't paid closer attention to the wave after wave of people offering their condolences. At the time, they seemed to blend together, but now she wished she had looked at them more closely. She had never seen anyone with her teal eye color except for her mom and her aunt. Her mom told her before it was a family trait. It was, most definitely, an unusual color.

"So, you're here and you're going to be living with Miranda, right?" The beautiful girl's voice was cold and harsh. Her voice seemed out of sync with her looks. Cory felt like a bucket of ice water had been thrown in her face.

She nodded.

"I'm Lilah, Lilah Werth. I am hopeful that you will manage your responsibilities now that you are with us."

Cory had no idea what she meant. What responsibilities? She felt Lilah's eyes travel over what was left of her faded Sharpie nametag. She watched as Lilah's lips curled in disgust over her appearance. Cory glanced towards Miranda who shook her head minutely.

"I will be watching, Cory Fall. Never forget that." The girl, Lilah, turned on her heel and walked away.

Cory's eyes widened. Why would she be watching? Why did she care anything about her? Why was she here today anyway? The only thing she knew for certain was that this girl with the teal eyes made her incredibly uncomfortable and she hoped not to run into her again. Ever.

In the car on the way home, Miranda cleared her throat. "Cory, I should tell you about Lilah." She took a deep breath. "Lilah, values honesty above all else. She is a little extreme about it."

Cory turned Miranda's words over in her mind. It was an odd thing to say and it didn't explain Lilah's demeanor or her words at all.

"You should know, she will be watching. She will be keeping a close eye on you." Miranda sighed again and silently stared out the window as she drove. Apparently, she was finished explaining Lilah Werth.

Cory felt more confused than ever. Who was she? Why would she be watching Cory? They had just met today, at a funeral. Why would she care what Cory did, ever? These questions had no answers that Cory come up with. As she contemplated, she began to wonder how they were related. They had to be. Their eye color didn't seem to exist outside the family.

CHAPTER 18

When they got home from the funeral, Miranda went to her room and shut the door. Cory sat in the living room for a while before deciding to take a hot shower. She wanted to think about the funeral and the parade of people who hugged and encouraged her when it was over. She needed a shower to think. She was afraid if she went to her room to paint or draw that she would zone out into her art. She wouldn't be able to think, she would disengage.

In the shower, Cory puzzled over the conversation she wanted to have with her aunt. She wanted to ask why there were so many people at her mother's funeral. Who were they all? What connection did they have with her mother? She wanted to know more about Lilah, and the people she felt sure were there with teal colored eyes. Could it be that she was related to them? Was she actually a part of a large family? A family she had never met and that she knew nothing about.

Cory wished she could simply sit down and have a conversation with Miranda. It would be awkward to pass notes and try to mime her many questions. But her tongue felt like it had atrophied from disuse. She wasn't even sure her vocal cords worked anymore. It had been so long since she had spoken.

She wondered if there was a point to her silence anymore. Sure, she was hurt unspeakably as a child, and at the time, not speaking made her feel safer. Now, not speaking made her life exponentially more difficult. Especially since her mother was gone, unable to stand by her, unable to tell others what she needed, unable to be her mouthpiece.

Cory's tears mingled with the water spraying on her face in the shower.

She had to be strong. She had to make something of herself. She couldn't continue to live life as this broken girl, unable to even ask for what she needed. She wasn't going to cry anymore, at least not where anyone could see her. She was going to be strong. She was going to be somebody who could take care of herself.

Cory knew with more certainty in her heart then she had ever experienced that she was going to live her life as a strong independent woman. She didn't need a group home. She didn't want to live with strangers like Ms. Grout the rest of her life. She was going to be an artist, have a studio, and she was going to make her own way.

She shut off the water and wrapped herself in her towel.

She needed to start speaking.

As she had the thought, she felt like her tongue instantly glued itself to the roof of her mouth in protest. Her mind flashed to Thomas and Jess from her old school. Their legs had been so extremely thin from never being used. She wondered if her voice had suffered the same fate.

It was going to be difficult to be the person she wanted to be, but it wasn't insurmountable.

She hoped.

In her room, she practiced opening and closing her mouth in front of the mirror.

She wasn't sure what to expect. It looked like her tongue still worked. Her mouth worked.

She could do it, surely it wasn't that much of a challenge.

As she considered whispering words to herself in private, her personal demons started rising up within her. Talking meant vulnerability. It would give others the chance to know what she was thinking, to get to know her. If they got to know her, they could hurt her. They could hurt her like he did.

"NO!" She thought to herself, "No, stop it!" Her mind screamed at her, the words dying off before they reached her vocal cords.

She was frustrated. She wanted to be able to speak, to be normal, but it was so difficult to break the pattern. She had to put herself out there and to overcome her personal barriers, but even thinking about it was more challenging than she had ever imagined. Right after everything happened with her dad, right after he tried to break her mother by killing her, she couldn't speak. It was months where she was physically unable to speak. Her mother, at her bedside the entire time.

Once she was physically healed, she could have spoken, but she didn't. She didn't want to. She didn't want to open herself up to others in any way. Her mother cared for her and made sure she always had what she needed. She didn't need to speak. Not speaking became her normal. It was safer for her to stay tucked away in her own head.

There had been so many therapists that tried to get her to open up. They tried to get her to speak to them, to her mother, to anyone. They wanted her to rehash her tragedy, so they could help her get through it, but she didn't want to. She needed to let it be, she worked through it herself in her mind and through her art.

In the years since it happened, she never wanted to speak. She didn't need to. Now she did. Now she had a reason. Her mom wasn't here. She needed to speak but she couldn't. Not yet anyway, but she wanted to, and she knew she would.

Soon.

She took a lined notebook and a pen from her backpack.

"Were they all family?" She wrote on the paper before setting out to find her aunt.

"Many of them were," Miranda answered after reading the note and allowing Cory to get situated on the bed next to her.

Cory wrote a large question mark on the paper trying to get Miranda to explain further.

Miranda sighed as if she knew Cory had more questions and she couldn't put off answering them forever, "your mother grew up in the area. She knows many people. Some were friends we grew up with, some were people she has known as an adult, but many were family."

She paused before explaining "she became estranged from all of us several years ago. She made choices to keep the two of you isolated. I was the only one from her past that she connected with for a while, but then we had the fight and that ended. You have to understand, that even though we didn't see you, nobody ever stopped caring for her or for you. They were like me, they have always loved you both even though we didn't always see things the same way."

Cory was stunned.

Miranda knew the questions wouldn't end unless she explained so she continued, "your mother made some choices that made some members of our family..." She hesitated as she searched for the right word, "uncomfortable, but your mother felt she made the right decisions for the two of you. She became disconnected with the family and everyone kept their distance, but that doesn't mean they didn't love you. No matter what happened, they loved the two of you and your mother loved them. They just couldn't be around each other."

Cory scrunched her forehead feeling more confused than ever. She silently encouraged Miranda to continue.

"I didn't," her voice trailed off as she closed her eyes. This conversation was obviously difficult. "I didn't agree with her shutting you off from the family. She felt it was necessary to keep you safe. After everything you had been through, it made sense. I understood where she was coming from even though I didn't agree with it. She made her decisions from a heart of love."

Cory sat as still as a stone statue.

"She wanted to keep you like a precious doll, locked inside a glass cabinet. She did everything for you. The only thing she wanted was to love and protect you. But, her protection has kept you from growing and from living."

Cory shook her head, but Miranda ignored her. "She let you waste away at a school you didn't need. She kept you from learning the things you need to know to be independent. I think she did it so you would always need her. You have been emotionally stunted and isolated, Cory. I told you before, it is what we fought about all those years ago. The way she chose to protect you is what we ultimately fought over. I thought she should push you into a normal life. She wanted to make sure you would never be hurt again. She did everything for you and never let you try."

"She wanted to keep you safe. She wanted to do everything for you. She facilitated you locking yourself away in your mind and your art. I thought you should be encouraged to live a normal life and go to a normal school. The thought of you being out on your own terrified her. It brought back all those horrible memories of what happened to you."

Miranda and Cory stared at one another, both

trying to harness their thoughts.

"As incredible as you are, Cory, you still need to learn how to be an independent person. You won't always have me with you. Your caseworker told me about the plan for you to stay at your school until you turn 21, and then they want to transition you to a group home.

"I know you can do better. I don't want that for you, Cory. I love you enough to push you. I don't want you to go to that school anymore. I want you to go to a regular school. You need it, Cory."

Miranda closed her eyes, letting herself get lost in memories.

She wanted to cry for herself, her mother, and her aunt. Everything seemed insurmountable.

She quickly wiped her tears and uttered a single hushed word. It was so quiet it was more of a sigh than anything else. "No."

Miranda, whose eyes remained lightly closed, never heard her whispered word.

CHAPTER 19

That night Cory tossed and turned in her bed, unable to let her mind quiet enough to find sleep.

She had stayed up listening to Miranda talk about the past, their family, and the benefits of her enrolling Cory in the public school. Cory wanted to be positive about it but everything was all so different and she felt inadequate and unprepared. She was terrified.

There were so many kids in a public high school and she really didn't know much about normal kids. She hadn't ever had a friend that would be considered normal. She wouldn't know anything about how to interact with any of them, much less be like one of them. She'd have to take classes about things she knew nothing about. They'd expect her to take tests and do homework. There was no way she could do that. She wouldn't even know where to start.

Her skin felt hot and wet, no doubt her fears were making her sweat. She threw her covers to the side and lay on her bed staring at the ceiling.

She tried to look at her situation objectively. She had recently been thinking about being more independent and someday living on her own. If that was her goal, shouldn't she try to learn something at school so she could function better as an adult?

Maybe, she thought, maybe it would work out okay. Going to school didn't mean she'd have to interact with anyone. She could just go, sit in the back, learn what she needed to know, and get out.

Independence and control over her own future were two things she desperately wanted. Yet, she would never have them if she couldn't prove to her caseworkers that she was capable. To be capable, she had to have some skills. She couldn't just hang out in the art room in a school for kids with special needs.

That night she told herself that she was going to be strong. This was her chance to prove to herself and everyone around her that she could do it.

She would try anyway.

If she failed, no harm done, she could keep the original plan Mr. Winter set up for her. She'd graduate and paint her life away in a group home. Maybe she could help out at the community art center if she had a handler to watch over her. Thinking about her future plans made her stomach roll with nausea.

Now that she thought she could try for more, she wanted it. She craved her independence, even though she knew it was going to be a battle. She had no real skills or knowledge to build on. She was beginning way behind the starting line. She had less than two years before she would turn eighteen before she had to prove to everyone she could do it. Was that even enough time? She had so far to go. But the alternative, if she didn't try, was so dismally oppressive. She had to give it her best shot.

Early in the morning hours she finally drifted off to sleep after she made a mental note find out when she and Miranda could get her enrolled in school.

Her eyes flew open of their own accord as soon as her room became lightened with the morning sun. Her resolve hadn't waned, but she was nervous to her core.

She took shower and tried to think about what she should wear. It wasn't like she had a ton of options, all of her clothes pretty much looked the same anyway. She was concerned because she wanted to be true to herself, but if she were being honest with herself there was a small part that wanted to be accepted at her new school. She tried to push that thought out of her head, she wasn't going to go to school to make friends. She only wanted to learn enough that she could gain her independence.

She pulled on a pair of black leggings, a black t-shirt, and a well-worn black hoodie that surprisingly wasn't covered in paint splotches. She gave a halfhearted attempt at brushing out her hair while she blew it dry. It looked okay down, but to be safe, she pulled a rubber band onto her wrist in case her hair got in her way later.

She stared at her reflection. Her smooth, clear skin was so pale. Her large teal eyes were both anxious and excited. She wanted to cake on her makeup to be ready for the day, but she was apprehensive about it. There was safety to her look, but she was changing.

How could she feel safe, be true to herself, and try for change? She studied herself in the mirror, then tweezed the few eyebrow hairs that had barely started to grow, smoothed pale foundation over her face, and with a heavy hand, traced her eyes with black kohl liner.

She was ready. Now all she needed to do was let her aunt know it was time.

She had spoken last night, only a single word, and her aunt didn't hear her. She wondered if the floodgates were open. Was she speaking now?

She wanted to.

Sort of.

Maybe.

She ripped out a scrap of paper and wrote, "I'm ready."

After making her way to the kitchen, she handed the note to her aunt who looked up at her in amazement.

"What, you are? You are ready for school?" Her shock was evident on her face.

Cory nodded.

"Okay. We can do this. Let me get dressed and we will go, okay?" Miranda was obviously flustered, it made Cory smile a little bit as she nodded again.

Cory poured herself a black coffee and stirred in a packet of hot chocolate mix. Then she made a slice of peanut butter toast and ate it slowly as she waited for Miranda. She felt nervous and unsure, but also a small part of her felt curiously strong. This was the first time she had made a big decision in her life, a decision that would affect her future. She liked the feeling.

The school was less than five minutes away by car. Cory figured she would probably be walking most days. She looked forward to the freedom of doing that simple act by herself. Overwhelmingly, she felt like she was making the right decisions.

The feeling faded as they pulled into the visitor spot at the front of the school. Dread threatened to overtake every emotion in her body. She pulled in a deep breath and resolved to herself that she was strong enough, she could do this, she would be a normal kid who goes to a normal school.

Her self-talk felt like lies. She forced herself to open the car door and walk into the building.

She didn't bother paying attention as her aunt filled out the stack of paperwork the secretary at the front desk handed her. Instead, she found a bench near the office where she could watch kids file in and out of the school. She saw how they playfully interacted with each other, spoke loudly, and wore colorful, fashionable clothes. Several of them gave her appreciative sidelong glances as they walked by. She desperately tried to ignore how fast her heart was beating. She was becoming more and more sure that attending a regular public school was a monumental mistake.

"Cory, could you come here for a minute? I think

you should hear this." Miranda's voice called to her.

"Hi Cory, welcome to Washington High. We are happy to have you hear and are certain you will get an excellent education." The secretary's words sounded like they were meant to be inviting, but Cory felt there was an edge of foreboding. She tried to smile but was certain she only managed a weak grimace.

"Why don't you come with me. We are going to have you meet with Vice Principal Cox and the guidance counselor, Mr. Rolf."

They were led into a small conference room just off the main office. Surprisingly, it felt almost familiar. It was like when Mr. Winter called her in for her future planning meetings. Those meetings were okay, she didn't really have to do anything. Maybe, she told herself, this meeting might be okay too. She tried to focus on her breathing to calm her erratic heartbeat. She was certain sweat was beading on her forehead, even though the room was somewhat cool.

The Vice Principal and the guidance counselor discussed Cory's history and past educational experiences. They were both certain that Washington High could meet her needs, but they insisted on her taking tests to know what classes to put her in.

Cory had sat in front of a variety of tests over the years. Usually, she doodled in the margins or tried to make a picture out of the bubbles on the answer sheet. She hadn't tried on her test in, probably ever. She couldn't remember taking an actual test where she tried, but she must have. It wasn't until third grade when she officially stopped trying.

She hadn't done much of anything since the third grade. Her teacher at the beginning of the year was Mrs. Sanchez. Cory remembered her as a nice lady that brought homemade treats every Friday if the class was good. She loved her.

She tried to remember more about third grade. She missed a lot of school because of her modeling, but she did well. She was considered smart back then. School was easy for her. But then, she almost died. Her recovery had taken so long, and when she was physically better she was locked inside her own mind. She didn't speak and the only time she held a pencil was if she was going to draw.

She quit trying in third grade. It was horrifying to her now. She wanted to be independent in the world with nothing but a third-grade education and an ability to create pictures on canvas.

She had so far to go. It was almost overwhelming. But she knew the alternative and she had to take a chance. It was her last chance. She had to force herself to be more. Even if she didn't manage much, she'd be better off than where she was today.

She wanted to ask when she needed to take the placement tests, but she wasn't ready to speak out loud. She had spoken one word to Miranda, but she wasn't sure if that really counted since she hadn't been heard. Asking a question in front of a group was way too far out of her comfort zone.

Although she hadn't actually asked, Mr. Rolf answered her question. "Cory, it is still early in the day and we would like to figure out where to place you. Could you stay and take some tests for us today?"

Cory's eyes were wide with apprehension, but she needed to get this over with so she nodded her acceptance.

"Wonderful. I will get you set up with your tests, then perhaps you'd like one our student ambassadors to give you a tour of the school. You could have lunch together and then your aunt could pick you up." He glanced at his watch and then at Miranda, "say 1:00 o'clock?"

Cory saw her aunt nod while she swallowed down the lump of fear in her throat.

She could do this, she chanted to herself over and over again as Miranda left and Mr. Rolf disappeared to gather the tests.

CHAPTER 20

By the end of her tests, Cory no longer felt as apprehensive about starting school. She simply felt brain dead. They weren't even as difficult as she imagined they would be. She was pleasantly surprised that she knew as much as she did, even though they took her awhile to finish. She wasn't used to reading or taking tests and she was a little slow.

It is what it is. She thought as she pushed her chair away from the table and started looking around for Mr. Rolf. She wasn't sure if he was planning to come back to check on her or if she was supposed to find him when she was finished.

She sat in her seat and fidgeted with her pencil. Then doodled a star design down the margin of her paper for a few minutes before giving up and deciding to look for him.

"Ah, Cory. You are finished." He took the stack of papers from her hand.

"Let's see if we can introduce you to our student ambassador and get you on the tour, okay."

Cory didn't bother to nod. Mr. Rolf wasn't really looking to her for agreement as he asked the secretary to have Tabitha Jones report to the office.

Cory examined the ends of her hair while she waited. She really needed a haircut. Then she picked at her nails thinking she would paint them that night.

She was getting restless waiting for Tabitha Jones.

She looked at the counter in front of the secretary. There were pens with fake red and yellow daisies taped to the ends in a mug that said, "I love teachers." She supposed the flowers were attached to the pens so people wouldn't steal them. She was wondering if she could borrow a pen to draw while she waited, but she didn't have any paper either. She considered asking for some, although, she knew she could just draw on her hand for a while.

Her thoughts were interrupted by Mr. Rolf's booming voice, "Miss Jones. Thank you for coming down. Let me introduce you to our newest student." He beamed a smile that showed far too many teeth. She figured he meant to flash a friendly smile and didn't realize that it came across as frightening.

Cory's gaze shifted toward the girl that entered the office. She was short. Maybe five feet tall and wore a pink and gray hoodie, dark blue skinny jeans, and gray converse high-tops. Her reddish-blond hair was pulled into a bun at the top of her head.

"Tabitha Jones, meet Cory Fall. Cory, this is Tabitha, our school ambassador. It is her job to represent our school. One of her duties is helping new students adjust. Tabitha, why don't you show her around the school and then take her to lunch in the cafeteria. Tomorrow will be her first official day."

Cory wondered why anyone would volunteer for a job showing new kids around. Plus, she was supposed to represent the school. Everything about the school ambassador job description sounded like torture. It made Cory wary of Tabitha's mental health.

"Actually," the girl said, turning a brilliant smile towards Cory, "you can call me Tabby. Everyone does. Where did you move from, Cory?"

Mr. Rolf cleared his throat and said, "Tabby, Cory doesn't talk much. She probably won't answer you."

Cory felt herself cringe in embarrassment at his words, thankfully Tabby didn't skip a beat. "Oh, okay, no problem. I am sure I can talk enough for both of us." She giggled like a happy child and smiled warmly at Cory who felt instantly more comfortable.

Tabby was diligent in her efforts to make sure Cory knew her way around the school. Unbelievably, she chattered amicably the entire time even though Cory didn't respond with anything except for an occasional nod or shrug. She wondered how Tabby found so many things to say to a stranger who offered nothing to the conversation.

She supposed everyone had their gifts. She found herself liking Tabby as she explained the layout of the school, who the good teachers were, and what kids did what.

Tabby had a stocky, muscular build. Cory wondered if she was a gymnast or perhaps a swimmer. She had numerous freckles across her cheeks and nose, and beautiful, shining green eyes. Cory felt unusually comfortable around her and thought she would make an interesting person to paint. She imagined the colors she would blend to get her strawberry-blond hair color right.

As they finished the tour of the library, the bell signaling the start of lunch rang. The halls instantly filled with students. Cory took deep breaths to keep herself calm and stayed close to Tabby's side. She wasn't used to so many students in one place.

They made their way through the lunch line getting sandwiches, apples, chips, and a drink before finding a crowded table at the back of the room filled with Tabby's friends. All eyes turned to study her as she moved to sit. Cory had to fight the urge to make a face, wanting to really give them something to stare at.

"Everybody, this is Cory. She is new here. She officially starts tomorrow. She doesn't say much so don't even bother asking. Cory, this is..." Tabby's voice continued to introduce everyone at the table, but Cory stopped listening, not even bothering trying to remember names. There were too many of them and their names and faces blurred together in her mind. Plus, she was never going to actually use them.

Quietly she sat at the table eating her lunch, watching the others around her. She noticed what they wore, what they ate, and who they talked to.

She could tell some were uncomfortable with her presence. Occasionally their bodies shifted toward her while their eyes snuck to covertly peek up at her. Cory had to fight back a smirk at their sidelong looks. It was funny to her how they tried to be sneaky, even though they were so completely obvious.

Tabby tried unsuccessfully to pull her into various conversations while the other students fully ignored her. Being ignored was okay with her. She wasn't attending the school to make friends.

Her eyes scanned the cafeteria, hoping to find a clock. She wanted to know how much more time she had at school before her aunt picked her up.

The clock hanging on the back wall had a silver cage around it. Evidently, the cage was in place to protect the clock from getting broken. It didn't work because the clock read 9:15 and was clearly not moving.

Irritated, she looked around the cafeteria, noticing the many tables of students surrounding her. They were all so loud and seemed to have their own spots where they fit in. She wondered if she would ever have a place where she would be comfortable. She figured she wouldn't be sitting by Tabby and her friends again at lunch, but she didn't know where she was supposed to go?

Her eyes searched the room in vain for an empty table. She wanted to have some idea where she could try to sit tomorrow.

Her eyes were drawn to a flick of dark hair, a perfectly cut shiny black bob. Next to her, a tall boy with caramel colored hair leaned down toward her to whisper something in her ear. His skin was flawless. His jaw angular. She had seen them before, but she couldn't place them even though she felt like she should be able to. It wasn't like she knew that many people, especially here.

She continued to watch the couple. There was something about them that she didn't understand and it was starting to get on her nerves. Their backs were facing her, but occasionally she caught glimpses of their profiles as they leaned to talk to each other.

"Well, Cory, the bell is about to ring and I should be going to my next class. How about I take you back to the office, your aunt should be there soon to pick you up." Tabby smiled sweetly. Cory appreciated the effort, she knew it must have been challenging to hang out with a mute girl all morning.

Cory nodded and pushed her chair back to stand. The chair toppled back with a horrendously loud clatter onto the floor. She was mortified as she hurried to set it right.

After the chair was righted, she looked toward Tabby hoping they could instantly disappear out the door. Out of her peripheral vision, she saw the couple she had been watching look directly at her. Now that she could see his face, she knew it was the boy was the boy from the art store. He was the handsome boy she had been sketching before her mom died. Cory's heart sped up as she made the connection, her eyes automatically shifted to the teal eyes of the beautiful black-haired girl next to him.

"Lilah," she breathed, shocked to see her again so soon and shocked that another word had spilled from her mouth. The boy made a move as if to stand. He looked like he wanted to come to her. Lilah placed her hand on his forearm, effectively stopping him.

CHAPTER 21

Cory had to hurry to keep pace with Tabby back to the office. As they made their way through the halls, she wondered anxiously if she would remember her way around the next day. A sense of unease bloomed in her chest as she thought about trying to navigate the school on her own.

"Okay, here you are. I will look for you tomorrow. You are going to do just fine. Well, I need to run."

Before she could spin around to make her way to class, Cory grabbed onto Tabby's arm.

"Thanks," she whispered, hoping her single word could convey how truly thankful she was that Tabby had shown her around and introduced her to her friends. Even though she was pretty sure she would never be one of Tabby's crowd.

Tabby smiled in response. "You're welcome, Cory. We are glad you are here." Tabby turned and disappeared back into the labyrinth leaving Cory feeling somehow lighter and less anxious in her wake.

Before she sat, she stopped at the secretary's unattended desk and feeling brave, helped herself to one of the flower pens in the "I love teacher's mug" and a piece of paper meant for students to use as a sign-in sheet when they were late to class.

She made her way to the still empty bench by the office and sat down. She flipped the paper to the blank back side and balanced it on her knee. Carefully, so she didn't push through the paper with her pen, she started to draw. She let her mind and pen wander. She let herself create a fantasy forest scene with a dragon sneaking around in the background.

She was so engrossed in her work, she didn't

notice that she was being watched until a warm body sat down next to her. He sat so close to her, she felt shocked and instantly moved as far to the side of the bench as she could. Her eyes darting toward the intruder.

She was met with bright blue eyes and a smiling face. "Hi." He said. "You draw really good."

Cory's fear dissipated as her body relaxed. This boy looked like he had Down syndrome. He looked like someone who would have gone to her old school and she found it reassuring. His face was curious and friendly. His dirty blond hair was a little too long and flopped into his clear blue eyes, causing him to push it back with his hand in an unconscious movement.

"I'm Jacob. I haven't seen you before. What's your name?"

Cory smiled warmly at Jacob and carefully drew a C followed by an ORY in block letters at the bottom of her drawing. Then she pushed the paper into his hand.

He looked carefully over her work and then said her name out loud. "Your name is Cory, right?"

She nodded.

"I like the name Cory. I like you and I like your drawing." He stated in a matter of fact tone.

She smiled and pushed the paper back at him when he tried to return it.

"For me?" He asked enthusiastically.

"Thanks." He said after she nodded her response. He held the paper in his hands and looked at it as if he had been given a precious gift.

"Cory, hi honey." She turned to see Miranda walking across the Lobby towards them. Cory stood, waved goodbye to Jacob, and caught up to Miranda.

It was nearly two o'clock when they got home. Cory felt happy but exhausted. She felt somehow empowered even though public school was going to be a major adjustment.

She went to her room and started blocking out a city from the perspective of someone looking down from the top of a skyscraper. She pulled out a palette and squeezed a blob of white and a slightly smaller blob of black. Her cityscape was going to be in shades of gray. To the side, she added small smears of red, blue, and purple to use as subtle tints.

It was almost eight when her aunt pulled her away from her work to eat. Miranda encouraged Cory to clean up and go to bed. She needed her sleep to start on her school adventure in the morning.

As she lay in bed, she tried to make herself relax in order to fall asleep. She had forgotten until then that she had seen Lilah at the school. She meant to ask her aunt about her. It seemed odd that she lived close enough to go to the same school. It seemed strange that she had family living in the same town, but her mom never mentioned them, and nobody ever visited. She hadn't even known they existed.

CHAPTER 22

Cory woke early. Somehow, she was able to sleep without tossing and turning all night. She was sure starting school would make sleep impossible.

As she showered, she felt herself growing increasingly excited and nervous about her first day. She felt like she needed some type of psychological armor to survive.

She dressed in a long sleeve black shirt under a short sleeve shirt with black leggings under a black above the knee skirt. Her skirt almost looked trendy with its short length. Even though on anyone else it would fall awkwardly under their knees.

She considered what to do with her hair. She liked to wear it long knowing she would be able to hide behind it if she needed to, but she hated the way it hung down her back like limp snakes. She ended up twisting it into a bun on top of her head, securing it with bobby pins.

She applied her thick, chalky foundation, covered it with ghostly powder, and circled her eyes with broad heavily stroked eyeliner. After her makeup was in place, she was ready to go.

The ride to school went by way too fast. Miranda asked if she wanted her to go with her inside. Cory's response was an exaggerated eye roll. Cory thought she saw Miranda try to hide a smirk when she did it. She wondered if Miranda secretly wanted to laugh at her response or was happy she was finally responding like a normal teenager.

Her apprehension grew as she made her way to the office. Somehow the school seemed bigger and more crowded than it was yesterday.

Before Cory could overthink her situation, the secretary called her over to her desk.

"Cory, glad to see you again. Are you ready?"

Cory nodded and tried to smile, but it felt mangled on her lips.

"Give me just a second, Mr. Rolf asked to talk to you when you came in for your schedule." She picked up the phone presumably to notify Mr. Rolf of her presence and then she handed her a schedule and a map of the school.

The schedule looked overwhelming. There was history 1, remedial math, English 1, health, art, and physical education. She wondered how she was supposed to manage getting to all of the classes in a single day. She took a deep breath and tried to reassure herself.

Mr. Rolf rounded the corner. "Cory, welcome back. I see you have had a chance to look over your schedule."

Cory nodded and looked expectantly at Mr. Rolf.

"Great, great. Listen, when it came to placing you in the right courses. We had a difficult time given your previous educational background and some inconclusive test results. I think we have a good plan for you, but we want to make adjustments if they are needed. It is always better to make changes sooner rather than later."

She scrunched the skin of her eyebrows and tried to give him an impassive questioning look even though his words were causing her anxiety to skyrocket. What did he mean? What was she supposed to do about it? Would she have to go back to her old school after she'd been trying so hard to be okay with this one?

"I'd like you to check in with me today after school. I'd like to know how your classes went. In addition, I will be tracking your progress with your teachers to make sure you are doing okay."

He seemed to sense her growing insecurity. "It isn't that I am worried about you fitting in here. On the contrary, you are just unique, and we want to make sure we are meeting your needs in the best possible way."

Unique. Why did he have to make the word sound like an insult? After all being unique is a good thing. Mermaids and unicorns are unique. It sounded like he meant to say misfit. Why didn't he just say misfit? She already knew she was one. He didn't have to sugarcoat it for her.

He seemed to be waiting for a response, so she nodded.

"Okay, then, I see you have your map. Your first class is down the hall on your left. Don't be afraid to let us know if you have any questions and I will see you after school."

With that, he turned to walk back to his office.

Cory had a bad taste in her mouth. Before she didn't have an opinion of Mr. Rolf. He was just an adult in her life, but now she was sure she did not like the man. She considered conveniently forgetting coming back to check in after school.

Her first class was history 1 with Mr. Jenner. She had never taken a history class before even though they did sometimes show movies about historical events at her old school. She wasn't sure what she should expect.

She took a deep breath and pushed her way through the door.

"Cory, Cory, hi, Cory." A familiar, happy voice enthusiastically greeted her.

She felt immediately relieved to see a friendly face in her first class. She forced herself to respond, "Jacob, hi." She managed.

She was amazed that, like yesterday, nothing earth-shattering happened when she spoke. She just talked like anyone else. Nobody made a big deal about it. It felt right.

The room was set up differently than she expected. The teacher's desk was at the front with a whiteboard behind it, but instead of rows, the desks were arranged so students would be facing each other in a circle.

Jacob took her hand and led her to an empty desk. "You can sit by me, okay. Nobody sits there, and Mr. Jenner won't mind. He's a good teacher Cory. You will like him, and you will get to sit by me. I know you like me because we are friends. Right, Cory?"

Cory smiled and nodded at him as Mr. Jenner walked toward her desk and introduced himself warmly. She was surprised at how comfortable she felt.

She had heard about the civil war, but she hadn't studied it before. She was surprised by how much she liked learning about it. Mr. Jenner was an engaging teacher who clearly loved his subject matter.

Jacob walked her to her next class, English 1. As he walked, he told her all about his girlfriend, Cleo, his pet turtle, Speedy, and his part-time job at a coffee shop. By the time they made it to her English class, she felt like she could use a break from Jacob. She genuinely liked him and already valued his friendship, but he was a talker and her ears needed a break from listening. She wasn't used to his chatter.

The rest of the morning went well, although not as good as history. She felt sure Mr. Jenner was going to be her favorite teacher.

She looked for Jacob at lunch, but couldn't find his blond head in the crowd. She was rescued from trying to find a place to sit by Tabby insisting she come back to her table. Since she had no other options, she agreed.

Lunch wasn't any better at Tabby's table than it was yesterday, even though nobody tried to secretly watch her out of the corner of their eye today. She knew she didn't fit in with her crowd but was grateful to Tabby for trying.

Eventually, lunch was over, and it was finally time for art class. Cory hoped above anything else that it could be her refuge the way it was at her old school. The way it was at home. The way it always was.

She was bumped and jostled in the hallway as she searched for and thankfully finally found the right classroom. She walked through the door just before the bell rang to start class. Idly, she wondered if she would ever get used to bells and schedules. It was hard to believe she was a student in a normal public high school. Before she didn't fit in at a school with 62 students, now she didn't fit in at a school with 960 students. It was hard to reconcile how much of her life had changed with how much had stayed the same.

She wondered if she would be able to graduate at eighteen or if it would take longer. It thrilled her to think there was even a remote possibility to be done with high school three years earlier than planned. As far as she could tell, she didn't seem to be considered especially special here. She was more like the dumb end of normal. Her math class was remedial, but the rest were just regular classes.

Every part of her wanted to graduate at eighteen rather than twenty-one. It was the first time she could see the benefit of trying in school and doing what she was supposed to do. Graduating at eighteen could be her goal. She'd do anything not to prolong her high school sentence.

She paused as she surveyed the art room. It was unlike anything she had ever seen. There were large blacktop tables with four stools around each one. The teacher had a large wooden desk covered in stacks of papers and a wooden artist's mannequin at the front of the room. The walls were covered in color wheels and random artwork. Cory guessed they were done by students. Some were decent, but most were formless and uninspiring. There were no windows in the room, the only light source was from the fluorescent bulbs in the ugly fixtures overhead. The worst part of the room was that it seemed overcrowded, every chair appeared to be occupied.

Cory took a deep breath trying to figure out what she should do next.

Thankfully, the instructor, Mr. Smythe, called out to her and found her a seat in the back of the room. She was thankful she would be sitting at the back. She looked around for the paint so she could get started, but was interrupted by Mr. Smythe.

"Hello, class. Today we are going to talk about pointillism. It came about as an offshoot of impressionist works. The technique is to paint using small dots of color that appear to blend together to create the composition."

Cory's mouth hung open as she sat through the lecture and demonstration of pointillism. By the time Mr. Smythe was finished, there were only fifteen minutes of the class period. There was not enough time to get started on anything, much less pull out paints.

Cory felt frustrated and wondered if art class was like this every day. No wonder, she thought, the student paintings on the wall lacked, well, everything.

She shook her head and pulled her backpack off the floor by her feet, setting it on the table in front of her. At least she could pull out a sketchpad and draw for a little bit.

"Hi there," a deep voice said from the table next to

her. She turned her face and studied the boy across from her.

He was decisively good-looking. He was tall and had the type of muscular build that would make a good model. She blushed at the thought. Luckily, he didn't notice because her blush was too delicate to be seen through her heavy makeup.

"I'm Damion." He said with an easy smile on his face. His skin was a flawless olive tone. His eyes deep brown, fringed with black eyelashes. His hair was longer, touching his collar. It was naturally very dark brown, possibly black, but difficult to know for sure because of the poor lighting in the room and because the tips of his hair faded from his natural color to a vivid blue. His black shirt had some band name she didn't recognize on the front. He wore silver rings with a tribal design on his thumbs and index fingers while the nails of pinky fingers were painted black. He wore black skinny jeans and black combat boots with purple shoelaces.

There was no doubt he was beautiful. His body, his face, his clothes were all gorgeous. His look was intentionally eccentric. She figured he was the type of guy who knew his charms and probably how to work them to his advantage.

She gave him a small half smile, turned back to the front of the room, opened her sketchbook, and started to draw.

He didn't seem to care that she was trying to ignore him.

"You must be new here. I know I would have noticed you before." He said.

Cory didn't acknowledge him.

"What's your name anyway?"

She didn't answer.

"Oh, the shy type, huh. Well, good thing I like the

shy type. In fact, I like the whole vibe you're putting off." She thought she heard a leer in his voice.

Cory glanced back at him in disbelief that he was still talking. She returned to her drawing and blocked him from her peripheral vision by resting her head on the arm closed to him, blocking him completely from her line of sight. She wished she had left her hair down, so she would have some sort of barrier between herself and this boy.

She heard a low chuckle coming from his table, but thankfully there were no more questions.

CHAPTER 23

By Friday, Cory felt like she was starting to settle into the routine. School wasn't as bad as she thought it would be. Her classes were difficult but manageable. Surprisingly, she felt a little regret that she hadn't been forced to continue her studies in a regular school at a younger age. Maybe if she had it wouldn't be so hard now.

But she couldn't blame anyone for what happened. She had spent so much time in the hospital recovering. There were so many tests back then. Nobody knew for sure the extent of her brain damage. Then when she didn't talk and refused to take academic tests, there was no choice except for special education.

Cory closed her eyes and shook her head. She had lied to everyone by not talking and not actively participating in her life. She knew that her brain was intact, even when she was little. It wasn't that she wasn't able to do things, it was that she didn't want to. At least not in the same way everyone else did. She wanted to shut herself inside her mind. She felt safer that way. So, she didn't talk. Besides, she always had her art to express herself. She didn't need words.

She was proud of herself for trying to talk now, but it was so difficult. She was out of the habit. The muscles in her mouth felt like they belonged to somebody else. She needed practice putting her thoughts into words.

She still hadn't spoken out loud to Miranda, at least not that Miranda knew. She wanted to, but when she did, she wanted to do more than grunt out a word here and there. When she spoke with her aunt for the first time, she wanted to be able to really talk. In order to do that, she would practice speaking before trying to have a full-blown conversation.

Her mind wandered. She knew she needed practice, but wondered how she was supposed to go about getting it.

"Cory, there you are Cory. I have been looking all over this entire school for you, Cory." Jacob's friendly face bobbed around her shoulder as they made their way down the hall.

Jacob would be the perfect person to talk to, Cory thought. She knew he already liked her and he wouldn't judge what she said or why she had issues in the first place.

Cory smiled at her decision to practice talking with Jacob. That way, when the time was right, she could talk, really talk, to her aunt. She looked forward to being able to do that. For a moment, she wished she had been able to talk with her own mom when she had the chance. She wished for a moment that she had been able to tell her out loud how much she loved her and nothing was her fault.

Cory shook away the regret and said, "hi." She wanted to say more, but couldn't force herself.

Jacob wasn't fazed. "Cory, I thought maybe you could come over this weekend. My girlfriend Cleo is coming over on Saturday afternoon and my mom said you could come to if you want to. Do you want to Cory? My mom said you could."

Cory looked into his pleading eyes, she wanted to say yes, but she needed to finish unpacking and she had to decompress from the week. More than anything, she needed to paint in order to collect herself.

She took a deep breath and tried to think of something that would get her off the hook, but wouldn't hurt Jacob's feelings. "Sorry. I can't. I am really busy this weekend." She managed and then forcefully exhaled. It was the most words she had spoken in years. She hoped she hadn't offended Jacob. She wasn't exactly lying, she planned to be busy even if she was only busy doing her own thing.

"That's okay, Cory. You can come over another time. My mom lets my friends come over a lot. We do fun things when I have friends over. Sometimes we play games, sometimes we play with my turtle, sometimes we eat ice cream. One time my mom took me and my friends roller skating and it was really fun. Maybe we could go roller skating sometime, Cory. That sounds fun, doesn't it?"

She giggled at his monologue and felt thrilled to have a friend like Jacob.

They entered the classroom and found their seats just before the bell rang. Unfortunately, Cory didn't have the chance to practice talking anymore that hour, Mr. Jenner was on a roll with his lecture.

She hoped she'd see Jacob at lunch, but she didn't. She ended up silently eating at Tabby's table again. She briefly wondered why she never saw him at lunch. This was her fourth day sitting at the table. Nobody said anything to her, but nobody made her feel unwelcome either. It was a little uncomfortable and she wondered if she should try to find somewhere else to eat.

She looked around the cafeteria not able to find anywhere where she could steal away to a quiet corner by herself. There were so many kids everywhere she looked.

She was glad when she was able to walk to her art class after lunch. It helped her feel centered even though her art class wasn't the free reign she had before. On Wednesday, she worried when Mr. Smythe took up almost the entire class period lecturing. It turned out Wednesday was the start of a new module and Mr. Smythe only lectured on the first day of a new module. For each module, he lectured and provided examples, then students were expected to complete a work in the same style.

It wasn't quite as freeing having to work in a prescribed style, but it was better than nothing.

Once in class, she pulled out the pointillism landscape in earth tones with brilliant fuchsia accents that she started the day before. It was something she would never have done on her own and she had to admit she kind of liked being told what to paint. Sometimes coming up with ideas was the hardest part.

She worked quietly until she realized it was time to clean up for the day.

"No, don't move," Damion ordered when she started to organize her things.

She couldn't help but glance at his table. He was turned directly toward her, pencil in hand, sketchbook open. He was drawing her.

She studied his drawing. He worked in a Japanese anime style. In his drawing, she sat perched on the stool, long legs gracefully entwined. She was holding the back of her neck. Her face was slightly raised and her eyes were closed. He captured enough of her Goth image along with her delicate features to make her look both strong and vulnerable. In his drawing, she looked exotic.

"Just another minute." He furiously sketched and shaded as he finished his drawing.

She felt strangely flattered as she considered him.

"Got it." He said. He closed his book and took two steps over across the aisle to her side of the table.

"You are a gorgeous model." He stated as a matter of fact. "I'd love to sketch you again sometime. Maybe somewhere outside of class."

Every muscle in her body seemed to lock down.

Damion leaned in toward her ear and whispered huskily, "I know you have this whole silent thing going on, but I got you on this."

She didn't say anything while she tried to ignore his warm breath on her cheek and focused on keeping her face frozen in an unreadable mask.

"I can see what you're thinking, and I know that you like me." He moved back to look straight into her eyes.

He was cute, and Cory felt flattered, but did she like him? She wasn't sure.

"I have news for you Cory Fall, but I think you already know what I am going to say." She had no idea what he was going to say. She looked down at her desk, trying to give herself mental distance from the hypnotizing dark eyes of the boy in front of her.

"I like you too, Cory. I like you and I always love a challenge." He reached over to gently stroke her cheek, he smiled, and turned to walk away.

Cory felt like she was spinning. Who was this boy and what did he want with her? What did she want with him? It was all so new, and she felt completely unprepared.

Her heart lurched. She felt an overwhelming urge to protect herself but wasn't sure from what. She felt so conflicted like she was going to hyperventilate.

The feeling stayed with her for the rest of the day. As soon as she got home from school, she started to pull out her paints, a palette, and a large canvas from under her bed. Her composition was going to be another self-portrait in black, white, and gray. It was going to be herself as jigsaw puzzle pieces completely disorganized with little chance of ever being put back together

CHAPTER 24

Just as she was going to squirt the thick black paint from the tube, her aunt knocked loudly on her door.

"Cory," she breathlessly started without any preamble, "I just got a call from a caterer about a wedding scheduled this Sunday. They had a family emergency and they have to cancel unless they get some major help." Her hair and eyes looked wild, Cory had no idea why it was such a big deal.

"Cory, I am going to beg you to help me on this one. This wedding is a huge for me. The bride and groom are important people in the community and if their wedding isn't perfect. I am ruined. I won't be able to book another client ever. I need your help. It is going to be a ton of work. I won't be able to pay you much, at least not until all the accounts are settled, but I will be so grateful. Please, Cory. Could you please help me this weekend?"

Cory shrugged her shoulders and then nodded. She wanted to unpack and paint all weekend, but she could help Miranda. Plus, she thought, if her aunt paid her at some point, she'd have money to buy more supplies. She was running a little low. She needed to figure out some way to get some cash.

"Oh, Cory, thank you so much. You have no idea what this means to me. We will have to go over there tonight and work on appetizers. I am going to need you to put your hair back. Tomorrow they will need you to prep as well and then Sunday you will need to help set up, serve, and then clean up. Do you think you can manage all that?"

Cory nodded again as she worked to twist her hair into a French braid.

"Oh, you will need a white shirt and a nice black skirt for the wedding. Do you have a white shirt?"

Cory wrinkled her nose and shook her head.

"Hmmm, I will have to look in my closet. I probably have something that will work. For now, let's get going, we have a lot to do."

Cory worked late into the night stuffing mushroom caps and rolling small pieces of ham around cheese and prepping trays of small pastries that wouldn't be baked until Sunday morning.

Saturday, she chopped and diced vegetables for salads and mixed some sort of artichoke stuffing for the chicken breasts.

Sunday morning, she set table after table with multiple utensils, small silver boxes of candy, and napkins folded into swans. She was exhausted by the time it was time to quickly shower and get ready to serve at the wedding.

Her aunt made sure to explain how she could not wear her usual makeup. Cory felt uncomfortable without it but only applied what Miranda would allow. Her skin was still pale, but a more natural color. She wore eyeliner, but it was an intentional cat-eye, not a black tunnel. She thought about drawing on eyebrows but decided it was okay not to bother. She felt like she didn't even look like herself as she twisted her hair into a sleek up-do to keep it out of her face and more importantly the plates of food she was serving. She was dressed in a white shirt, black pencil skirt, black pumps, and she was ready.

She worked hard at the wedding setting plates, clearing plates, refilling glasses, and smiling at guests. The bride looked beautiful and the guests looked to be having a good time. She was sure this wedding would not go down as a disaster for her aunt's business.

She smiled as she thought about her help with the

successful wedding just as a camera flashed in her face.

She blinked away from the light and then scrunched her eyes toward the source.

"Sorry," the photographer said before turning to take pictures of guests on the dance the floor.

Miranda chatted animatedly that night on the drive home. The wedding had gone flawlessly, her reputation was intact.

Cory was happy for her aunt despite her aching legs and heavy eyelids. All she wanted was to sleep.

CHAPTER 25

"**H**i, Cory." Jacob greeted her from his seat in history class. "How was your weekend? Was it as busy as you said it would be?"

Cory felt guilty for a second because of how she hadn't exactly told Jacob the truth on Friday when he asked her over. On the other hand, it turned out she wouldn't have been able to go to his house anyway. She ended up being way too busy. Just like she said she would be.

In the end, she hadn't lied.

Weird.

"Yes, Jacob it was crazy. I worked all weekend."

His eyes got large, "You did. I didn't know you had a job. I have a job too, in the coffee shop. I like working at the coffee shop. I clean the tables and the floors. I even know how to make a few kinds of drinks. I worked on Sunday. Did you work on Sunday too?"

"I did." She smiled at Jacob.

"That is so cool, Cory. We were working at the same time." He pushed his fist toward her for a bump. She obliged.

Jacob was interrupted by Mr. Jenner walking in and starting to talk about Fort Sumter. Despite his status as her favorite teacher, she wasn't paying attention. She was thinking about her discussion with Jacob. She was pretty sure what they had just said to each other counted as a conversation. At least she was going to count it as a conversation. She had done it and it felt good. Good enough to almost count as natural.

The content feeling that she had since she spoke with Jacob dissipated later as she walked behind two of the kids that she usually sat by at Tabby's lunch table.

They had seemed to like her well enough. Even though they had never tried to talk to her, they smiled when she sat down every day. She thought of them as friendly acquaintances.

"I am hungry." She heard the girl with the long brown ponytail complain.

"Me too. I can't wait for lunch." The blond girl responded.

"Ugh, lunch. I hope that weird chick doesn't sit with us again."

"I know. What is her deal anyway?" The blond girl whined.

"It's Tabby. She likes to take on lost causes." The brown ponytail giggled.

"Yeah, well good for her," Blondie said in a condescending tone. "Does that mean the rest of us have to suffer along with her?"

She didn't hear the rest of the conversation because she slowed her steps in order to put some distance between them. She thought the others didn't mind her presence, but she understood now. She wouldn't subject herself to them anymore. She could take a hint, even if it was unintentionally given.

Cory sat through her next class trying to decide how she was going to handle the lunch hour. She had a few crackers in her bag. She had them in there as an emergency snack, but they would be enough to tide her over. She decided when the bell rang she would sneak outside and find somewhere quiet to eat.

"Hi, Cory," Tabby said, catching up to her in the hallway after the bell rang. "Come on, I'll walk with you to the cafeteria."

Cory didn't want to be a pity project. "Actually, I brought a lunch. I am going to eat outside today." In an instant, she decided the crackers counted as a lunch.

Tabby stood gaping. It was the first time she heard Cory speak a full sentence. She was shocked.

Cory said nothing else as she swung her bag over her shoulder and headed to an outdoor bench along the side of the school.

She knew Tabby's friends weren't hers. She knew she was a misfit in so many ways and that lunches in the cafeteria were uncomfortable at best. At the same time, she thought there were parts of her that were fitting in. Hearing what those girls said brought the truth home, she would always be the oddball. People didn't really want to be around her.

She dug into her bag for her crackers and was surprised by the brown paper lunch sack she didn't know was there. Inside, there was a cranberry juice, a turkey sandwich on a soft croissant, and a large red apple.

She felt so thankful when she ate. She had no idea how Miranda had known she'd need a lunch. She had never packed one for her before.

The sandwich was delicious, exactly what she would have asked for if she had ordered it from a restaurant. She took a swallow of her cranberry juice, her favorite kind of juice when the tall boy that she had seen in the art store and again with Lilah approached.

He was so good-looking, she felt paralyzed.

"Hi." He said in his deep, masculine voice. "Can I join you?"

She didn't have a hope of being able to form words, not to him. He was too cute for ordinary conversation. She felt her heart start to race as her trembling hands gestured to the empty side of the bench.

"I'm Jaxson. Jaxson Harper." He said.

She didn't respond. She was at a loss for what to do. She wanted to introduce herself, but couldn't form the words. She thought about taking a bite of her sandwich but was sure she would choke on it if she tried. So, she sat like a statue awkwardly holding her juice, her half-eaten sandwich balanced on her thigh.

He cleared his throat. She wondered if he felt as awkward as she did.

"I've seen you a few times." He finally said. "This might sound strange, but I have been thinking about you since the first time I saw you in the art store. I've been feeling like I have to talk with you. I have to get to know you." He stared at her in unblinking earnest.

Cory was stunned. His words were shockingly intense. She had no frame of reference for what to do or say.

They sat awkwardly looking at each other.

"I'm friends with your cousin." He finally managed before adding, "Lilah."

She really didn't know how to respond. She didn't know Lilah and had only recently found out they were related. Besides they were shoestring relatives at best, not first cousins. At least she didn't think so.

He looked at her face. His mouth opened and closed again. It seemed like he wanted to say something else, but wasn't sure what.

His pale blue eyes were mesmerizing. Cory couldn't help but study the contrast between their light color and the bronze of his skin. He was beautiful.

"There you are." Her voice echoed off the school wall.

Her eyes flicked away from Jaxson's face to Lilah fluidly making their way toward them. Even at a distance, her teal eyes were flashing with an intensity that surprised Cory. She wondered if her eyes ever looked like that. It was surreal seeing her own unusual color on another person.

"I am ready to eat, Jaxson. I have our lunch. Come with me." She ordered.

Jaxson seemed torn while Cory quickly shoved her

half-eaten lunch back into the brown sack and gestured for Lilah to take her spot.

"Has she said anything to you?" Lilah snapped at Jaxson while ignoring Cory.

Jaxson shook his head in response. Was it her imagination or did he look disappointed? Lilah seemed to take a deep breath before directing her attention to Cory.

"It's for the best you know." She said as she took her now empty spot next to Jaxson. Cory gave her an inquisitive look. "It's for the best if you never speak again. It makes things easier."

Her teal eyes locked with Cory's. "Not speaking is the best way to keep secrets. Unless, of course, you are dead."

Her voice was cold and full of authority. Cory was too shocked to respond. Her mind was spinning with confusion over what Lilah could possibly mean. She had a strong desire to tell her off, but she couldn't. Not yet anyway. It was still so difficult to put her thoughts into actual spoken words. Especially with him looking at her. Someday she would tell Lilah exactly what she thought, but for now, she needed more practice.

Cory shrugged her thin shoulders and started to walk back into the building. She wanted to appear unaffected and indifferent. She didn't want Lilah to think her words had any effect on her. Still, she couldn't stop herself from glancing over her shoulder at the pair.

Lilah was organizing their food. Jaxson was staring at her, with a look on his face that she couldn't interpret, watching her walk away.

CHAPTER 26

Her appetite was gone so she slipped the rest of her sandwich into her backpack for later. She didn't know what to make of Jaxson or Lilah other than they must be dating. She had only seen them in the cafeteria once. She wondered why Jaxson approached her the way he did. Did he want to get to know her because she was Lilah's cousin? Maybe he wanted brownie points for getting to know her family.

She snorted at the thought. She was pretty sure Lilah wouldn't be impressed if Jaxson became friendly with her.

For some reason she couldn't identify, she felt conflicted.

Lunch wasn't over, but she couldn't bring herself to go to the cafeteria. She snuck into her art class, thrilled the room was empty. She needed to start on her painting.

Even though she had mostly finished her pointillism landscape, she couldn't bring herself to fully complete it. She had no patience for the tiny dots, especially not today. She needed broad strokes and thick bands of color.

She examined her landscape and decided it would be interesting if she painted in the edges of her landscape in a realistic form and then let them fade into pointillism. It wasn't exactly what Mr. Smythe asked them to do, but she didn't care. She'd take whatever grade she got. Right now, she just needed to paint.

She organized her colors, selected the brushes that would allow the thick lines she needed, and filled a cup of water for her brushes.

With sure strokes, she brought her vision to life. It was still a landscape, earth tones accented with intense fuchsia. The left third of the painting was stylistically real but abstract. Then it became slightly fuzzy becoming more and more dotted in impressionistic dots.

While she was lost in her painting, she didn't realize the room had slowly filled. Students took their seats and watched her work. She was inspiring in her precise strokes and focused intensity completely unaware of her surroundings. Soon, her classmates pulled out their own paintings to quietly get to work.

Mr. Smythe stopped short when he walked through the room. There was something different about the class today. Usually, the room was filled with chattering students barely paying attention to the work in front of them. Today, the room was quiet, students were diligently studying their paintings and thoughtfully choosing their colors.

He meandered through the room offering critiques and suggestions, before stopping at Cory's table to watch. Her drawing met his criteria for the assignment, but that wasn't what he observed. Her painting had an energy of its own. Cory didn't seem to be aware of his presence or that she was in a school art room. She was lost in her art.

She was surprised when the bell rang, pulling her out of her haze. She was shocked she had been so oblivious to the time and was upset about being late to her next class.

"Let me help," Damian said as he took her painting to place it in the drying rack. She washed her brushes while he wiped off her table.

"Thanks." She breathed as they headed out of the classroom.

"Anytime. You were incredible today by the way."

He said, nudging her shoulder with his own.

She smiled at him unable to say anything else.

"Would you like to get together after school today?"

"For what?" She asked, feeling flattered, but confused.

"I thought we could do homework or maybe work on some drawing." He said smoothly.

She wasn't sure what to do. Part of her wanted to go with him. She should work on homework. She was starting to like him. Every day he made a point to talk to her even though she never responded. He was beautiful to look at, but she wasn't sure she wanted to be alone with him.

Damian could read the conflict across her face. "Come on, we'll go hang out at the community center by the library. There will be people everywhere. What do you say?"

It was only a few weeks ago she was thinking about going to a different community center to help teach art, but only if she had an aide with her to make sure she could handle it.

She had come so far in such a short time, and she was doing everything a normal kid would do. She felt a surge of pride.

"Yes." She said, feeling uncharacteristically confident. "I'll go with you."

He smiled as they made plans to meet after school.

Her afternoon dragged on minute by minute. She was apprehensive about meeting Damian, but meeting him at the community center felt right. She hadn't been able to turn him down when he mentioned going there. She felt like she was symbolically closing the door on who she used to be. She didn't need an aide to go watch over her while she went to the center. She was going to the center because she could.

She made the choice to go and she loved that she could. Not talking was the only other independent choice she could remember making in her life. She loved feeling like she had control in her own life.

"Cory, hi, I am glad I caught up with you," Tabby said as she walked up to Cory while she waited in the lobby for Damian.

"Listen, I heard some talk at lunch today and I am afraid some of it may have gotten back to you." Tabby looked like she wanted to cry.

Cory reached out to give her arm a reassuring squeeze.

"I want you to know, you are welcome at my table anytime. I want you to be happy here and I want to help you."

Cory sensed that her heart was in the right place, even if Tabby did see her as a project to be fixed.

"I am not sure what you heard Tabby, but really I am doing fine." Cory was trying to sound sincere, but she wasn't sure how to do it. Conveying emotions through words was foreign territory for her.

"I know you have to eat somewhere and I am so sorry if some of my friends made you feel less than welcome. I have to apologize for them. Why don't you and I eat together at a different table from now on, okay?"

Cory was touched that Tabby would offer, but she would never feel comfortable with her leaving her friends for her. She had to say something to let Tabby off the hook. She tried to think fast.

"Tabby, I am really doing fine," she began, but she could see the doubt on Tabby's face. "Besides," she hastily added, "my best friend, Annaliese, is going to transfer to this school. I will have her to eat lunch with. Please don't worry about me." Cory tried her best to sound convincing even though she had no idea what made her say Annaliese would be transferring to the school.

"Really, that is great news! I am so happy for you. But Cory, please know, I am a friend too. I will be there for you if you need me, okay?"

There was something about Tabby that was so trustworthy. Cory got the sense that she really was someone who wanted the best for others. She was happy to count her as a friend.

As she stood waiting for Damian, she felt more and more horrified by her lie. Why would she say something like that to Tabby? It was true she'd love to have Annaliese at her school, she probably was her best friend even though that was only because the only other friend she had was Jacob and maybe Jess from her old school. Annaliese probably barely remembered the strange Goth girl that stayed with her for a few days of emergency shelter.

Cory shook her head. She was embarrassed that she would lie outright to Tabby about something that will easily be proven a lie when Annaliese doesn't enroll in the school.

She stood berating herself, wondering how long she could wander the halls at lunch avoiding Tabby. Maybe, she thought, if she could stay invisible long enough, Tabby would forget about her and her fictional best friend.

Her musing was interrupted by Damian's approach.

"Hey, are you ready?"

She smiled and nodded.

Damian carried on a one-way conversation on the way to the community center, telling her all about his love for anime. He wanted to go to college for digital arts and maybe be an animator someday.

They found a comfortable pair of blue vinyl club

Embellish

chairs in a quiet corner near the window.

"I am glad you decided to come with me today, Cory. I have been trying to figure out a way to spend time with you."

She smiled but said nothing.

"I know I said we could do homework, but I was hoping you'd let me draw you."

"Only if I can draw you." She said, surprising them both with her response.

"I'd be honored Miss Fall." He said in a husky voice. She pulled out her sketchbook and a small tin of pencils and erasers.

"Can I see some of your work?" He asked when he noticed the well-worn pages of her book.

"Maybe someday if you play your cards right." She was shocked by her own words. It sounded like she was flirting. Was she? She wasn't sure, but for some reason, she felt suddenly both shy and exhilarated.

She decided to be finished talking for a while. Talking seemed to get her into trouble.

She pulled her legs up onto the chair and folded them underneath her. She carefully balanced her sketchbook between her knees and the arm of her chair before turning to study Damian's features.

She had known he was handsome. Now that she was really looking at him, she saw how the intensity of his expression enhanced his decisively masculine features.

She studied the way his arm fluidly moved across the page as his eyes narrowed slightly scrutinizing her, and the set of his mouth as he captured her image.

As if in a trance, her hand started to glide across her own sketchbook blocking in his image on the paper. He sat forward in the chair, looking up, trying to understand how her features fit together. His body was relaxed but controlled. He was trying to capture her on paper the same way she was trying to capture him.

They said nothing as they alternated between studying one another and their paper. She was trying to shade and contour with a ferocity. She rubbed her thumb across her lines occasionally trying to blur them together. After blending, she worked the image over again with the tip and then the side of her pencil. She needed to get the play of light across his face just right. She built up the marks only to go back and take away parts, giving his form the right depth on the paper.

His lines were stylized and gliding, alternating between thick and thin. His lines were alive, taking away detail to focus on the critical elements. He studied, drew, and then flipped his page over. He didn't seem unhappy with his work, it was more like he needed more. It seemed like he was trying to burn her image to his mind and capture her subtle expressions on paper.

They were both breathless from their intense focus when Cory's phone pinged with a text. The sound reminded them where they were and what they were doing. Cory blinked rapidly to pull herself back to reality. Damian grinned over at her.

The text was from Miranda, letting her know she was outside waiting for them to finish up.

"That was incredible, Cory. I've never done anything like that before. Let me see yours."

She smiled and held out her drawing. His face and body were nearly perfectly recreated in pencil. The light and dark of his features made the drawing look like a photograph, while the background was barely blocked in making it fade inconsequentially into the background.

"Wow," he breathed in astonishment, "incredible."

He held his book toward her. Her breath caught as

she saw herself over and over again with slightly different expressions. True to his favored style, she was a captured as a work of modern art. Her images were sexy, menacing in her gothic style, but feminine and alive. She wanted to see herself painted in grayscale with the background in vibrant hues.

She stroked the sketchbook and smiled flirtatiously at him. He responded by closing the distance between them. He reached his fingers forward to brush her face gently from her temple to her chin.

She stood frozen, waiting to see what he did next.

Since she didn't pull away from his touch, he leaned forward to graze his lips across her cheek. "I am definitely into you, Cory Fall." He whispered.

CHAPTER 27

Mr. Jenner stood at the front of the class rubbing his hands together in front of him. His jubilant expression was infectious. It made everyone in the class unconsciously sit forward in their seats waiting to hear what he had to say. "Okay everyone, I know I have told you that a civil war project was coming. Usually, we write 5 to 7-page papers about a battle of your choice." His eyes twinkled as he smiled conspiratorially.

The class groaned in unison, slumping back in their seats.

"But wait," he sounded like an infomercial about to announce the top-secret buy one get one free offer that everyone knew was coming. "This year we are going to do something different." His smile was radiant. "This year, we are going to have you work in pairs to present a significant event that occurred in the civil war."

Cory wanted to crawl under her desk and then keep going to head out the door. She couldn't present; she had just barely begun to talk. She tried to come up with a plan where she did not have to have a partner. That way she could just not do the assignment and happily take a zero for a grade. She felt green; she had been working so hard to get decent grades. She hated to lose it all, but she didn't feel like she had a choice.

"Your presentation," Mr. Jenner continued, "can take any form you want. You can do a PowerPoint, you can do a skit, you could write a book, you can make a video, you can do whatever you want to creatively present your event. You will only have 10 minutes to do it, so you have to take that into account, but other than that, the sky is the limit."

Maybe it doesn't have to be so hideous, Cory tried to reassure herself even though she felt miserable.

The class burst into whispered requests for partners and discussion about what to present.

"Cory," Jacob stage-whispered into her ear, "you want to be my partner, right? I think we could do a really good job. I want to do a good job. I like to present in front of the class. I am pretty good at it. Everybody says so."

Cory's heart soared. She was thrilled to have a partner. She didn't even care if he was good or not as long as he did the standing up in front of the class part. "Yes, Jacob, we can be partners."

They talked for a while about what event they could take before settling on General Lee's surrender at the Appomattox Court House. Jacob was really into the drama of between the North and South before Lee eventually surrendered. Cory could tell Jacob would be happy putting on a one-man play about it.

"I know you don't like to talk much. Why don't you do a drawing, a really, really big drawing?" He held his arms out wide before continuing, "then I could tell everyone about it. That would work for a presentation, right?"

"What if we take a giant roll of banner paper and draw in where everything took place in Appomattox? It would be like a huge map. Then you could tell everyone about what happened while you point out where it happened."

"Yeah, that would totally work, Cory. Could we make the banner so big it goes all around this entire room? Then it would feel like we are really there."

Cory laughed. "How about we see how much paper we can get?"

They couldn't get paper as large as they wanted,

but they did get enough that it spread across the front of the room. They rolled it tightly and secured it with rubber bands. Cory wanted to get thick markers for the drawing because the lines would be visible, easy to work with, and she'd be able to make it colorful.

They didn't have time to start the project during the class period, so they made plans to go to Jacob's after school to work.

At lunch, Cory wandered the hallways, trying to appear like she was walking with a purpose. She didn't want anyone to question her about why she wasn't in the cafeteria. Luckily, nobody seemed to notice her. She wondered how long she'd be able to lurk in the hallway at lunch before getting caught.

She went directly to the art room at what she thought was an acceptably early time. She figured she might have to say something to Mr. Smythe as an explanation, but since she hadn't been there for the entire lunch period, she thought he wouldn't mind too much.

She was surprised to see Damian when she entered the room. He sat back at his desk working intently with markers. She didn't see Mr. Smythe, and she suddenly felt shy being alone with Damian.

She quietly walked up to him, peering at his paper.

He was adding color to the drawings he had done of her yesterday. He had outlined parts of his drawing with a black marker to refine and draw attention to his lines. His added backgrounds of intense color made her look like a superhero. She loved it.

"Those are awesome, Damian." She said, without worrying about using words, who she was talking to, or what she sounded like.

Damian looked up into her eyes and smiled. "Glad you like them." He said. "I had fun yesterday, you know. I was sort of hoping we could do it again today."

Her face clouded over. "Actually, today isn't a good day. I need to work on a history project with a friend."

"History project?"

"Yeah," she giggled, "I need to work on a nearly life-sized map of Appomattox, Virginia."

"Sounds extreme." He teased.

Her heart felt like it was going to explode. She wanted nothing more than to be near him. She wanted to talk to him. Most importantly, she felt like she could talk to him. Like a normal girl talking to a normal boy and she loved the feeling.

Soon the room started to fill with students, Cory returned to her seat to start working on a new class project.

Her hour of art was over far too quickly, she wished she could simply skip her afternoon classes and stay in the art room until school was out. Skipping classes to do art was one of the things she missed about her old school, but she was starting to feel so much more normal here. The best thing was that she didn't feel like she was losing herself in the process. She felt like she was becoming a version of herself that had possibilities. She had choices that she had never had before. Having a say in what happened to her was the part of normal that she craved. She was going from black and white to full color.

Before the bell rang for the end of class, Mr. Smythe called Cory to his desk. He wanted to meet with her after school.

"Today?" Cory squeaked. "Today I can't. I am meeting someone to work on a history project."

"Cory, this meeting will be quick, but it is important. We really do need to make it today, right after school in Mr. Rolf's office."

"What, Mr. Rolf's office?" She choked on her words. She was shocked their meeting had to include the school counselor. It felt like she was having a massive case of déjà vu, like she would be walking in on another future planning meeting. Her face burned with frustration. She thought she had been doing pretty well all things considered. She hadn't even complained about how short her art class was, at least not out loud.

After agreeing to go to the meeting, her afternoon was spent anticipating the worst about what would happen when she got there. She didn't think Mr. Smythe wanted her out of her art class, but she worried that he might. She couldn't think of anything she had done that would get her kicked out of school, but maybe she had. She didn't really know all the rules, maybe she had done something unforgivably wrong without knowing it.

She felt flustered by the time the final bell rang. She hurried to the office, hoping to find out what the meeting was about so she could be put out of her misery.

Mr. Smythe and Mr. Rolf took their time getting to the office and then they made unending small talk once they did find their seats in the small room. Cory felt like she might burst out of her skin if they didn't tell her why the meeting was called. She had prepared for the worst and she needed them to get it over with.

"Cory, thank you for coming in this afternoon." Mr. Smythe said, unofficially calling the meeting to order. "I wanted to talk to you about your art and I needed to make sure it happened in time for us to meet some critical deadlines."

Cory's mind raced. She didn't think she'd missed any assignments, but maybe he wanted her to turn something in from before she enrolled in the school. It didn't seem fair, but it could be possible.

She didn't bother trying to form a coherent

question. She just looked quizzically between the two men.

"Cory, you have exceeded our expectations. I am so pleased that you are doing so well." Mr. Rolf proudly beamed like he had something to do with how she was doing in school. Cory tried not to grimace at his arrogance. She didn't want to consider that he might actually be responsible for her doing well. He did, after all, create her class schedule.

"Cory, your pointillism landscape demonstrated incredible artistic talent. I was hoping that, with your permission, we could enter it in a statewide competition." He paused, seemingly waiting for her response. She didn't give one.

"The winner of the competition will receive a full ride art scholarship to the University. I think you have a good chance of winning, but we have to turn in your work tomorrow. I need your permission to enter." He seemed apologetic when he added "normally we prepare students and work with them on their submissions. They usually enter two or three pieces, but since you have only recently started at our school, we didn't have the time. Unfortunately, at this point, we are rushed, but I wanted to make sure you were able to participate. Even if you don't win, it will be a learning experience that you could use to enter next year."

Cory felt the air leave her lungs in a rush. She was officially blown away, having never considered college. She never thought she was capable. Even if she had been interested and wasn't a special ed student, she wouldn't have gone because was she didn't have the money.

What would her life be like if she went to college?

If she went to college, there would be no doubt in anyone's mind that she could be independent.

Her head was spinning, and her heart rate surged. The thought of living her life has an independent person thrilled her. Living on her own doing art was a million times more appealing than living in a group home hiding supplies and doing art.

"Yes." She said in a strong, clear voice. "Yes, please enter my work in the competition. Thank you."

CHAPTER 28

After the meeting, she rushed to meet Jacob. Jacob was pacing anxiously just inside the front door to the school.

His face lit up when he saw her walk toward him.

"Cory, I am so glad you are here!" He yelled enthusiastically. "I was afraid you forgot about us. That would have been too bad if you forgot about us, Cory. We have a lot of work to do on our project!"

She grinned at him. "I could never forget about you, Jacob."

"Come on, my mom is waiting outside to take us to my house. We can have a snack when we get there. My mom makes really good snacks. Then we can work on our project, okay?"

She nodded and followed him to his mother's running car parked three spots from the front door.

The pleasant looking blond woman did a double take when Cory approached. She seemed taken aback that her son would be friends with a Goth girl. He obviously hadn't told her what she looked like. Thankfully, she skillfully covered her initial reaction.

"You must be Cory. Jacob has told me a lot about you." She said in a soft pleasing voice.

"Yes, hi, Mrs. Anderson. Nice to meet you." Cory intentionally practiced her manners, not having done so out loud in years.

Jacob's mother seemed to relax as she listened to Jacob and Cory interact on the drive home.

They ate tomatoes, cucumbers, and chocolate chip cookies when they got to his house. Jacob only wanted the cookies, but his mother said he couldn't have them unless he ate the vegetables first. Cory smirked at their

169

interaction.

After their snack, he turned on his laptop and pulled up maps of Appomattox and what happened during the civil war. They studied the maps while Jacob made notes for their presentation and Cory sketched ideas in her notebook for their banner.

When they were finished, Cory tried to figure out how they should sketch in their banner. She wanted to make sure the proportions were right. There wasn't anywhere to stretch out the entire paper at once, except outside, and she didn't want to get the paper dirty.

They ended up unrolling the banner so it was open about three feet in the middle. They set it on the kitchen floor. Cory studied her sketches to determine where everything should be placed and then started blocking in what would be in the middle of their banner. As she finished that section, they unrolled the banner to the right with Cory sketching more and more of the landscape. When the right side was finished, they rolled it back to the middle of the drawing and repeated the process to the left.

"Cory, we did awesome on this, you know that right? I don't think anybody will make anything as good as ours."

She laughed because the only thing Jacob had done on the drawing was help roll and unroll the paper as needed, but it did turn out fairly awesome.

"Yeah, Jacob, we did." She responded as she put the rubber bands over their 33-foot banner to keep it in place.

They sat on the kitchen floor while Jacob read over the facts he wanted to include in their presentation. Although they had casually talked about what to say, Jacob was the one that had organized the talk.

She was impressed. "Jacob, you are really smart.

You know that, right?"

"Yeah, I know I am smart. I know I have Down syndrome, but I am just a regular guy. I go to school. I go to work. I have friends. I think I do pretty good. I don't really get what all the fuss is about, but sometimes people think I can't do things before they even know me and that makes me mad. It makes me want to show them, because I can, Cory. I can do things."

"I know you can, Jacob. I've seen it." She uttered with sincerity. He had to work a little harder than most people, but he was happy to do it. She felt inspired to work harder by being around him.

Cory left that night with promises to finish their map. She felt light and happy like she could do anything. Tonight, she decided, was the night she was going to talk with her aunt. She wanted to tell her thank you for all that she had done and how much she appreciated the push to enroll at her new school. If it weren't for Miranda, nothing would have changed in her life, but now, everything was different.

She got home to a dark house; Miranda obviously wasn't home. Cory vaguely remembered her aunt telling her she had some sort of dinner meeting where she would be previewing a band. She shrugged her shoulders; their conversation would wait. Whenever they got to it, she would be ready.

The next day at school, she got some work done on her poster in history. She tried to give Jacob a marker and coach him in how to fill in her images.

She quickly realized Jacob didn't like to draw or color. He preferred sitting near her and keeping her company by talking.

It surprised her that he didn't like to do art; she didn't understand why he wouldn't. It was so natural and relaxing that she had a hard time imagining anyone not loving it. Even so, she kind of liked that he didn't want to work on the banner. It meant she could control the outcome.

In art class, Damian hung around her desk. He said he didn't have ideas for what to work on.

"You know I had fun the other day at the community center."

She smiled coyly at him as she looked up from her sketchbook.

"I was thinking maybe we could go there again."

She nodded in agreement.

"Maybe we could go this afternoon, after school."

"I'd like to." She started, "but I need to work on my banner. I need to get it colored."

"You know I am an expert color-er don't you?" He gave her a half smirk.

He would do an excellent job, she thought. Plus, she'd love to spend more time with him. "I don't know," she pretended to think, "what are your qualifications?"

"Maybe, I could show you some of my work, like a portfolio." He said silkily.

She waited expectantly in silence.

He reached under his desk to get his sketchbook from his backpack.

He flipped through a few pages before coming to one of her. She sat perched, legs crossed under her, looking up from the page. Her frame was delicate, her teal eyes, outlined in black, were extra-large and commanding, her bold red lips appeared contemplative. There was a sketchbook on her knee and a pencil in her hand. Her black hair a solid mass curling past her shoulders. The three-dimensional background was done in reds and purples.

She loved it.

"Wow." She breathed. "That is awesome."

He placed his hand gently on top of hers. "Thanks. I had a beautiful model."

Neither one said anything for a moment before Damian broke the silence, "so how about the community center tonight?"

"Yes," she said without hesitation, "I'd love to."

After making arrangements to meet, Cory floated through the rest of her classes. She was really starting to like Damian. He seemed so genuine, he liked art as much as she did, and his looks were unbelievable.

They found their corner of the community center empty again. Together, they pushed the chairs out of the way and proceeded to lay the banner on the ground in front of them so they could work on the poster section by section.

They drew and colored until the banner was finished and the markers almost completely dry. When they stood to pack away the banner, Cory's back, neck, and knees were sore from her crouch. She closed her eyes to stretch her back.

Her eyes flew open when warm hands started rubbing at the knots in her shoulders.

"Mmmm, that feels so good. Thank you."

"Of course," he answered. "I should be thanking you for letting me come here today."

She snorted indelicately, "Are you kidding, after all the coloring you did today? I owe you big time."

He just smiled confidently at her. "Maybe you do owe me."

"Definitely. You are officially my hero."

"I don't know about hero status, but I know one way you can make it up to me."

She looked at him quizzically. "And how is that?"

"You could come to the fall formal with me." He stated.

Cory's nonexistent eyebrows raised. She didn't

know how to answer. She had never been to a dance or on a date. The thought terrified her, but she did like Damian. Maybe if she went out with him it would be okay.

"So, is that a yes?" He asked nudging her arm playfully.

"Ummm ... yeah. Yeah, I'll go." She said shyly and then gulped.

"Come on. It isn't going to be that bad. In fact, I think you might actually like it" With that, he took hold of both her upper arms and pulled her toward him before leaning down to capture her lips with his own.

His lips were soft and warm, gently moving over hers. She closed her eyes wanting to get lost in the sensation. All too soon, it was over.

That night, she dreamed of the kiss and of Damian.

CHAPTER 29

The coffee shop was just a couple of blocks past the school. Miranda was always busy with weddings on the weekends and Cory didn't mind walking. She held the banner carefully as she meandered her way to meet Jacob when he finished work. She knew she would be early and she wanted to kill a little time before she got there.

Her original plan was to spend the weekend painting, but when Jacob asked her to come over, she didn't have the heart to tell him no two weekends in a row. Besides, they did need to go over their presentation a few times before class on Monday.

Despite her leisurely pace, she still managed to arrive at the coffee shop thirty minutes before Jacob was due to get off work. He saw her as soon as she walked in the door. As soon as their eyes met, he smiled and waved the mop handle he was holding at her.

She ordered a large orange ginger mint tea, added a packet of artificial sweetener, the kind her mom always told her to avoid and sat down at a partially hidden corner table to wait. She propped the banner in the corner next to her chair and held her tea carefully in her hands for a few minutes letting the cup warm her fingers. It smelled delicious, but even without even a sip, she knew it was too hot to drink at the moment.

Setting her tea on the table, she reached into her bag for her sketchbook. She groaned as her hand fished through her belongings. She forgot that she had taken her book out of her bag last night. Her bag contained her markers, a tin of drawing pencils, a pair of sunglasses, a library book, and an apple.

She looked around the coffee shop for some loose paper that she could at least doodle on. The only thing she could find to draw on was napkins. Unfortunately, her markers bled through the insubstantial paper while her pencil lines couldn't mark heavy enough without ripping the paper.

She sighed and looked around. She still had over 25 minutes to wait and that was if Jacob got off on time.

She rolled up her sleeves, pulled out a fine point black sharpie, and laid her left arm on the table. She began to draw an intricate spider web from her left ring finger to her elbow and all around her forearm. She studied the design for a moment, then added a small black spider between the second and third knuckle on her left ring finger.

She had gotten so caught up in her drawing, she stopped paying attention to the activity around her. She hadn't noticed anyone coming or going and because she was so quiet in the corner, nobody had noticed her.

As she sat examining her forearm, she heard a chuckle that surprised her. It made her look up, searching for the source.

Her first reaction was to smile because it was him. Damian.

She felt silly because she thought she might have swooned.

Her first instinct was to go to him, but then she saw he wasn't alone. Damian was sitting next to a girl. Their chairs were pushed so close together they were touching. She was beautiful with her poison green curly hair, tight black t-shirt, blue plaid skirt, knee-length white socks, and black combat boots. Cory watched in horror as he leaned in to kiss her behind her ear. It struck her how comfortable they were touching and cuddling in public.

Cory felt sick. She wanted to run and hide, but she also wanted to show him that she was strong and independent without him. He was one of the few people she'd opened up to. She had kissed him and liked it. She was planning to go to the dance with him. She had no idea that he already had a girlfriend or at least someone he was comfortable kissing behind the ear in a coffee shop. She was disgusted.

Of course, she tried to tell herself, spending time with one another and going to a dance together didn't mean they were exclusively dating. Her logical side knew that they hadn't had the conversation to define what they were to one another. But in her heart, she thought they were together. It hadn't even occurred to her to question what was going on between them. She thought he felt the same way she did.

She felt shattered. How could she feel so good yesterday and so horrible today? She knew nothing about dating. Why did she think she could try? She wasn't normal, had zero experience, and nobody to talk to. She wanted to lock herself in the bathroom and cry, but she wouldn't. At least not here and not now.

He hurt her, but she wasn't going to hide. She hadn't done anything wrong besides maybe assume she meant something to him.

She took a deep breath, walked to their table and took a seat in the chair directly across from the couple. She didn't say or do anything except lean forward, placing her elbows on the table, her chin resting on her hands, and stare at them.

The girl looked confused. Damian looked caught.

Cory closed her eyes for a moment and summoned her strength. She felt like a fragile flower that had just been crushed, but she wasn't going to let her feelings show. She was angry at herself for letting herself care so much for Damian so quickly. He was the first guy she'd had any sort of relationship with and that let him get under her skin. They were barely dating. They had hung out a few times and had plans to go to a dance. She wouldn't let herself be crushed; she would be strong. After all the things she had survived in her life, she knew without a doubt that she was strong.

In a clear voice that surprised herself more than anyone else, she said "Damian, I don't want to go to the fall formal with you anymore. In fact, I don't want to be around you at all anymore."

"Cory," he spluttered obviously searching for the right thing to say.

There wasn't a right thing he could say. She was about ready to return to her table when the green haired girl snapped "you were going to the dance with her? You were planning to go to the dance with the freak and not me?"

Before any of them could say anything, the girl pulled the rounded plastic top and straw off of her caramel-colored drink and dumped it over Damian's head. Then she whirled on her heel and stomped out of the coffee shop.

Cory stifled a laugh, briefly wondering what specifically made her more of a freak than the green haired girl. Damian's eyes bulged as he patted himself ineffectively with a stack of napkins. He tried to splutter an explanation for what he was doing and something about the dance that she didn't quite catch.

Cory didn't want to hear what he had to say. She had seen enough. She held up her hand to him to signal him to stop. "I don't want to go with you. Besides, I am going to the dance with someone else."

He stopped patting his head with the napkins, "what? You're going with someone else, but I just asked you."

"Yeah, I changed my mind." Cory had no idea why she was lying other than the fact she wanted to look strong in front of Damian. She wanted to look like she wasn't hurt.

"Who are you going with?" Damian barked.

Cory's mind was blank. Of course, she couldn't think of anyone she'd be going to the dance with, but she had to say someone's name, otherwise, he would know she was lying. She would look pathetic and she couldn't let that happen. With a racing pulse, she blurted out, "I am going with my boyfriend, Jaxson Harper. We are dating. It's new. You and I, we are nothing. Nothing ever happened between us."

She knew she was blushing uncontrollably, probably visible through her makeup. She couldn't believe what she had just popped out of her mouth. Why would she tell Damian she was going to the dance with Lilah's boyfriend? Worse yet, she said that they were dating. It was the worst move she could have made. He was surely going to find out about her deception. She was just so angry, she couldn't stop the words from coming out of her mouth.

She stood and walked back to her table, feigning nonchalance. Internally, she cursed herself for not making up a name or giving the name of anyone from her old school. It would have been better if she stayed silent. Staying silent meant that nobody really knew what she was thinking, and she never had to explain herself. She felt tears of frustration prickle in her eyes.

Without looking, she reached into her backpack for her sunglasses. She needed to hide her eyes. She had to make herself look calm and unaffected. She picked up her now warm tea and started to coolly sip as Damian slunk out of the coffee shop.

CHAPTER 30

Thirty minutes later, Jacob loudly slammed into her chair. "Hi Cory. I'm done with work now. Are you ready to work on our project? Wait, are you taking a nap? I didn't think you were, but I don't think you moved in a long time and with your sunglasses, I can't see if your eyes are closed."

In spite of her mood, she smiled at Jacob's chatter. "I'm not asleep, Jacob. I was thinking," about how stupid she felt about Damian. "Yes, let's go work on the project."

She had been sitting still for a long time; her legs were stiff when she stood. She shook herself out before throwing away her cup and gathering her things.

She and Jacob walked to his house. She was sulky and wanted to be home in bed feeling sorry for herself. She knew she wasn't the best company for Jacob, her heart wasn't in it. Luckily, Jacob didn't seem to notice, much less be offended. He was easy for Cory to be around. He effortlessly carried on a one-sided conversation that only required an occasional laugh or comment. It almost made her feel like her heart hadn't been ripped to shreds only hours ago.

She didn't tell Jacob about Damian. It was too complicated, and Jacob would for sure have questions. Cory didn't how she'd answer them. It wasn't like Damian was her boyfriend, she'd just felt like they were headed that way. She was afraid if she had to answer questions from Jacob, she might break down in tears. That would be embarrassing. It sucked being sixteen and completely new to any kind of interpersonal relationships.

After a while, the discussion turned to their

presentation. They decided they would stretch the banner across the front of the classroom and hang it with masking tape. Then Cory would sit down, and Jacob would do all the talking. She didn't really care what he said, as long as she didn't have to do it. He pulled out several pages of handwritten notes. She watched as he practiced reading from his notes and pointing out on the banner where events happened. If he was able to do the presentation the way he practiced, they were going to do well on the assignment. For some reason, she didn't understand, Cory was excited to do well in school.

Jacob's mom gave her a ride home when they were finished. Cory could feel their eyes on her back as she walked toward her front door. She turned and waved goodbye before letting herself into the empty house. Her time with Jacob had kept her mind off Damian, but now that she was away from him and alone in her house, her contentment faded.

Miranda would be working until late that night and Cory had nothing to distract her. She never liked to watch TV and she wasn't much of a reader. Tonight, she didn't feel like working on her art. She needed supplies anyway. Miranda didn't have a cookie jar of cash for her to dip in to when she needed things.

Cory was frustrated. She pulled out a tub of ice cream from the freezer and sat to eat it directly from the container with a spoon. The weight of the day seemed to bury her. She felt so dejected. She was angry at herself for liking Damian so much that she felt hurt at all. Plus, she was irritated that she needed art supplies and didn't have any money.

She needed more to do.

She thought about getting a job. She could see about working in the coffee shop with Jacob. Or maybe she could ask Miranda if she knew of a caterer who needed regular weekend help.

She felt a slight glimmer of hope as she finished the ice cream. She would love to have some sort of steady income and maybe she'd like having a real job.

After her shower, she braided her hair so it wouldn't be horribly tangled in the morning, and went to bed.

Her sleep was fitful. Unfortunately, her mood hadn't improved by the morning. She still felt off. Miranda was home, puttering around the house, but Cory didn't feel like talking with her. She stayed in her nest of blankets and stared at her ceiling for quite a while before rolling out of bed to eat her breakfast in silence.

The day felt too long. She didn't bother changing out of the old sweats and t-shirt that she had worn to bed. She didn't have the energy to pull out her sketchbook. She just sat in her room feeling like mush. To make matters worse, she was disgusted with herself for feeling the way she did. She wished she could snap herself out of it.

The doorbell rang late in the afternoon. She didn't move to answer it.

"What are you doing here?" She heard her aunt ask.

"I am not sure. I have to talk to her." A female voice said.

Cory strained her ears to try to listen but didn't care enough to get up from her bed to find out who Miranda was talking to.

"Nothing has changed." Her aunt insisted.

"Something has. I feel it. I just don't know what."

Then there was silence before Cory heard footsteps coming toward her room.

She was surprised to see Lilah standing at her door. Lilah wore perfectly fit low rise blue jeans and a short sleeve green sweater that had a scooped front that showcased a silver dragonfly necklace. Her sleek black hair seemed to be slightly disheveled. Lilah didn't cross the threshold, instead, she remained in the doorway and stared down at Cory.

Slowly Cory sat up on her bed and blinked her eyes toward her intruder. She didn't feel like talking to anyone right now, especially Lilah.

"Cory, I need to know what is going on," Lilah demanded in a no-nonsense voice.

Cory didn't alter her stare.

"Lilah, really. Nothing has changed. I am not sure why you had to come here today. I told you I would call you." Miranda came into view behind Lilah and tried to placate her with a soothing voice. It struck Cory as a strange thing for her aunt to do. It was almost like Miranda was afraid of Lilah, but that didn't make sense.

Lilah ignored Miranda and took two steps into the room. "Cory, Jaxson told me he was going to the fall formal with you." Her voice was full of accusation.

Cory's eyes widened, and her heart started to race. She told Damian she was going with Jaxson to the dance because he was the only guy she could think of. Did Lilah know she lied about going out with her boyfriend? Damian wouldn't have told her, would he? She felt stunned and mortified. She couldn't believe her stupid lie had gotten back to Lilah so quickly. She mentally berated herself for not coming up with any other name. She had been so stupid.

"He said nothing about taking you before. When did he ask you?" Lilah asked threateningly.

Cory had nothing to say. There was no way she could get into the explanation, not with Lilah glaring at her.

"Or," she continued in a low, hostile voice, "did he ask you?"

There was something in her question that disturbed Cory. Cory tried not to move a muscle, not even to breathe.

"Of course, he asked her if she is going to the

dance." Miranda scoffed. "Cory doesn't speak. You know that. There is no way..." Her voice trailed off as her eyes flicked questioningly towards Cory. Cory had the distinct impression that she was missing something.

Lilah waited, lips pursed and hands on hips, for Cory to say something. It was as if the three of them were frozen in uncomfortable silence.

Lilah finally broke the tension with a huff. "Let's get this straight, Cory Fall, I know something is going on. I don't like it. I will be watching, and I will intervene if I need to."

Cory wondered if there was something wrong with Lilah.

"Lilah, why don't you stay for dinner? Maybe if you spent some time with," she paused briefly before finishing her sentence, "us, you would get to know Cory a little better. Then, maybe, you wouldn't be so worried."

"That won't be necessary." She glared toward Cory and turned to march out of the house without another word.

Cory's heart was still racing, embarrassed to be confronted by Lilah of all people in a lie. Miranda gave her a small smile before mumbling something about making dinner and leaving the room.

Cory tried to think about what she could do to make things better. She didn't ever want to see Damian again. Of course, he said something, but she didn't know why. Unless he and Jaxson were friends. It was the only explanation that made sense. She had never seen them together, but that didn't mean anything since she didn't really know anyone at the school.

She supposed she could be brave and talk to Jaxson and tell him what she did. She could explain what she saw and how she used the lie to save face. The thought of confessing to Jaxson was nauseating. She couldn't even say hi the other day. There was no way she could get through an embarrassing conversation.

There was no one that she could go to for advice. She couldn't talk to Tabby about what happened; she would be too worried that she'd tell someone and her embarrassment would be spread around the school. She couldn't talk to Miranda because she'd want her to talk it out with Lilah and possibly Jaxson. Jacob was out because she wouldn't want to do anything to bring his happy spirit down to her confused level. She wished Annaliese was around. She would understand and maybe even have some advice on what to do.

Her sleep that night was disturbed. She kept tossing and turning, unable to stop her brain from thinking. She worried about Jaxson humiliating her by telling everyone she deluded herself into believing that he'd go to the dance with her. Lilah's threats to watch her repeated over and over in her thoughts while Damian snuggled the green haired girl in the background of her mind. When she did sleep, she dreamt of Jaxson and Damian laughing together about her thinking she had a chance with either of them.

She woke up in a sweat before her alarm clock.

Thankfully, her solution had come to her in her sleep. She had to drop out of her new school. It was the only thing she could do. Nothing good could happen for her if she continued to go there. She should have never opened her mouth to talk. She should have refused to take the placement tests when she started at her new school. She should have stayed mute and refused to participate. Then they would have had to let her stay at her old school. She had been happy there.

She couldn't stay at her new school. Everything she did was wrong. She would have to talk to Miranda.

CHAPTER 31

She showered quickly. Her mind was racing as she tried to figure out the best way to talk to Miranda. Then she pulled on the same sweats and t-shirt that she wore to bed the night before and then snuck downstairs to make coffee. She only occasionally drank it. She didn't particularly like the flavor, but on days like today, she desperately wanted the extra push she hoped it would give her.

She drummed her fingers on the counter as she waited impatiently for Miranda to wake up. She was nervous about the conversation she wanted to have; she had to get her aunt to agree to let her go back to her old school. It seemed like the only way things could go back to normal. She was worried about what Miranda would say. She also wondered if she would still be eligible for her old school once they knew she could talk and that she could manage classes at a regular school. She quickly made the decision to worry about school requirements after she convinced Miranda to let her go back.

She drank two cups of coffee while she waited for her aunt to get up. Actually, it was more like two half cups of coffee and two half cups of milk mixed with a lot of sugar. The result was a lukewarm drink with an only slightly disgusting flavor. By the time she finished her second cup, she had the feeling her heart was fluttering like a hummingbird. She wasn't totally sure if she had the feeling because of her low caffeine tolerance or because she was dreading the discussion she wanted to have with Miranda.

The house remained still as Cory sat at the table waiting.

After another ten minutes, she decided she better get ready for the day. She went to her room to dress and apply her makeup. She paused before she got her eyes done. Maybe she didn't need the black circles today, maybe she could try to highlight her eyes with her makeup instead of canceling them out. Maybe she would feel more powerful if she looked her best. One thing she knew for sure was that today she needed all the power she could get.

She carefully used her eyeliner pencil to outline her eyes and add a dramatic wing effect. It was a lot more than most people would wear but almost nothing for her. She liked how it brought attention to her stunning teal eyes. She outlined and filled in her lips with a plum colored pencil before sweeping her hair into a messy bun on the top of her head. She frowned at her sweats and changed into black skinny jeans, a black tank-top, a well-worn black t-shirt with a loose neckline over it, and her doc martens. The spider web she drew along her left forearm on Saturday at the coffee shop while waiting for Jacob had faded into a faint but discernible design.

She liked what she saw in the mirror. She tilted from one angle to another. She looked good, different, but good. She still looked edgy, but less freak show. Somehow, she felt ready for the change.

She gave her room a half-hearted cleaning but stopped when she heard shuffling sounds from the kitchen along with cabinet drawers opening and closing. Miranda was up.

She took a deep breath. She was apprehensive about what she had to do. Talking with kids at school felt safer for some reason. Talking to Miranda was more important. Instinctively, she felt like once she spoke to Miranda, she wouldn't be able to retreat to the safety of silence. Silence was security for her and it would be gone.

Cory steeled herself for what she was about to do. She was ready to change. She had to prove herself by talking to Miranda. She tried not to think about how much she wanted change and independence, even though her plan was to beg Miranda to go back to her old life and her old school. Even though she knew if she went back, she would be different. She would go back, but it would never really be the same. This time she would have the power of speech.

"Miranda, can I talk to you?" Cory asked quietly after she entered the kitchen.

Miranda gasped in shock and fumbled the bag of bagels she held in her hand. "Cory, what, when did you, oh my gosh." She was almost incoherent as she ran to grab Cory in a tight bear hug, burying her head in the crook of Cory's neck.

Cory's lips curled into a smile as she let Miranda's arms squeeze around her. It felt warm and secure. Neither of them said anything more for several minutes until Miranda loosened the hug and pulled away dabbing at the tears clinging to her lower eyelashes.

"Honey, I am so proud of you." Her voice breaking with love and admiration. "When? What made you decide? How?"

Cory giggled at her aunt's confused questions before answering truthfully, "Since I got here. It has been a little at a time. It's been difficult, but I made myself practice at school. I've gotten better."

"I am so proud of you," Miranda repeated. "Your mom would have been so proud."

"Thank you," Cory whispered as her own eyes began to mist.

They stood facing each other, holding each other's hands. Suddenly Miranda's expression changed from devotion to concern and then for an inexplicable reason, Cory thought she saw fear. "Cory, there is one thing you must always do. You must always tell the truth. Do you understand me?" Her voice was full of alarm.

"Ye...Yes. Of course," Cory stammered, wondering why her aunt would feel the need to give her such a strange warning. Miranda looked worried.

"Miranda, I need to talk to you about going back to my old school."

"What? Why?" Miranda asked.

"I just need to. I feel like it would be better. I'd have more time for my art." Cory tried to think of an excuse that would appeal to an adult. She didn't want to tell Miranda how she lied to Damian right after her aunt begged her to always tell the truth and she couldn't face people in her new school again. Not after she'd screwed everything up.

"That's ridiculous, Cory. You need more than just art. Plus, you have come so far at this school, a normal public school. Look at you, you have only been there a few weeks and already you are talking and you did it on your own! It's incredible, really." She said, brushing off Cory's plans to change schools.

"I just really want to go back, Miranda. Please?" Cory begged, even though the thought of going back to her old school and her old life made her stomach want to hurl. She had nothing there, no choices, no friends. Nothing but solitude, a few classes that were ridiculously easy, and art. Now that she knew she could, she wanted more from her life.

"Absolutely not. Now Cory, hurry up and get your things. I am going to drive you today or you will be late." Miranda's eyes were hard. She obviously had no desire to continue the conversation.

Cory saw the way Miranda's jaw set as she spoke

and knew she wouldn't be switching schools anytime soon. She couldn't help but let out a growl of frustration, even though she had to admit, going back to her old school wasn't as appealing as she tried to make it sound to Miranda. She was going to have to suck it up and face Damian, and probably Jaxson and Lilah. Maybe, she thought, she could go back to being mute, at least at school. It was certainly safer. She wouldn't say anything to embarrass herself.

She slowly turned to get her backpack. Luckily, she saw her banner propped next to the door as she left the room. She had completely forgotten about her presentation with Jacob that morning. He would have been devastated if she wasn't there for it, especially because she had the banner. She couldn't leave him hanging.

Cory sighed. She was dreading the day, but she had to get it over with.

She hurried out of Miranda's car and ran to Mr. Jenner's room as fast as she could. She made it to class seconds before the bell rang. Jacob didn't seem to notice that she was out of breath and not listening as he described his weekend.

Jacob stopped chattering, faced forward, and raised his hand as high as he could the instant Mr. Jenner asked if there was a volunteer group ready to do their presentation. Cory merely smiled and shook her head at Jacob's enthusiasm. She didn't care when they presented because she wasn't planning to say anything anyway. Her contribution to the project was over. It was out of her hands and she didn't really care.

He pumped his fist like he won a prize when Mr. Jenner called on him and told him they could go first.

Mr. Jenner helped Jacob stretch the banner across the front of the room while Cory taped it in place before returning to her seat. She sort of felt like she should take a bow or something to show that her part was over. Mr. Jenner looked at the colorful banner approvingly before giving Jacob the signal to start.

Jacob smiled brightly and went through the presentation in a loud clear voice, hardly needing to refer to the notes in his hand. He enthusiastically pointed out different spots on the banner to illustrate what happened just before the courthouse surrender. He did even better that morning than he had when they practiced on Saturday. Cory clapped loudly and fought the urge to stand when he was finished.

Jacob did take a bow when he finished. Then he flashed Cory a smile so wide it almost split his face. Mr. Jenner asked if he could keep their Appomattox banner because he wanted to use it the next time he taught about the civil war. Jacob looked mildly distressed about giving up the banner but quickly agreed when Cory shrugged her shoulders.

Jacob gave her a fist bump when he came to sit back in his seat. "It's okay if he takes our banner, right Cory, because you could make another one if you wanted to. You could just draw whatever you want to draw. Maybe we could do it at my house again. That was fun wasn't it Cory?"

"Maybe we could draw something else next time, okay, Jacob?"

"Yeah, something else is good." He opened his mouth to speak but had to stop because the next group was ready to get started.

During the next group's presentation, Cory started to plan how she was going to avoid Damian, Jaxson, Lilah, Tabby, and Tabby's friends. So far, her plan was to avoid the cafeteria during lunch. She thought if she walked the school halls like she had somewhere to go, she wouldn't look like she was killing time. She didn't think anyone would really notice her and she wouldn't get in trouble. She would be able to hide in plain sight.

After class, she navigated the crowded halls toward her locker.

"Hey, Cory," Tabby said, leaning on the locker next to her as she put her books away.

"Hey, what's up?" Cory responded.

"I just gave your friend a tour of the school. It is awesome that she transferred here." Tabby said as Cory looked at her with a blank expression.

Cory waited a beat for Tabby to further explain. When she didn't, Cory said, "I don't know what you are talking about." She felt honestly confused. She didn't have friends. She had no idea who Tabby could be talking about. She must have her confused with someone else.

"Your friend, Annaliese. Today is her first day." Tabby looked at her like she was being purposely slow on the uptake. Cory was, after all, the one who told her about her friend transferring to their school. Impatiently she added, "I gave her a tour this morning. She is taking tests with Mr. Rolf as we speak so they can figure out her classes for tomorrow."

"Annaliese is here?" Cory asked, dumbstruck.

"Yes," Tabby hissed, looked slightly irritated. "She said something happened in her foster home. I don't know what, she has just been placed with a family who lives close to here, and today is her first day."

Cory instantly worried about what could have happened at the foster home. She had only been there a few days, but they had made a big impact on her. She truly cared for Annaliese and the boys. Of course, she could live without Ms. Grout, but even she hadn't been that bad.

"I need to see her," Cory told Tabby.

"Well, you can't. She's taking tests. Come to the cafeteria with me." Tabby responded with a smile.

"No, I will wait for her in the lobby." She turned to walk toward the front of the school as if in a trance she said, "I can't believe Annaliese is here."

Out of the corner of her eye, Cory saw Tabby shrug her shoulders and presumably turn to make her way to the cafeteria.

Cory found her bench near the office and made herself comfortable. She assumed Annaliese would be taking tests with Mr. Rolf, the same way she did. She couldn't believe Annaliese was really here, enrolling in her school. It seemed so unlikely. She wondered if Tabby got something wrong, maybe it was a different Annaliese starting at her school.

She hoped her friend was the one who would be going to the school. She was excited for Annaliese to be there, but also a little nervous. She considered Annaliese her friend. She'd never exactly had friends before and by default that made Annaliese her best friend. She wondered if Annaliese would consider her anything more than an acquaintance. A stranger she slept beside a couple of nights in foster care once.

Cory decided it didn't matter; she had to talk to Annaliese.

She glanced at the clock and noticed that lunch was already halfway over. Cory wondered if she should skip art to wait for Annaliese. If she skipped art, she wouldn't have to see Damian and that wasn't a bad thing. She didn't want to see Damian, but she didn't want to get in trouble either.

She closed her eyes and leaned her head against the wall. She was going to wait for as long as it took. She had to see Annaliese.

Fortunately, it didn't take long. She heard Mr. Rolf's deep timber coming from the office about test results and class placements, just as he had done with her when she started. She felt a giddiness steal through her. She was excited to have Annaliese at her school.

The door opened, and Annaliese stepped out nodding to Mr. Rolf as she said goodbye.

Cory jumped up and raced over to her friend. She looked a little different. Her hair was no longer fire-engine red. It was a deep burgundy color like the drawing Cory had done of her.

Cory giggled and held up a lock of hair. "I like it." She said.

Annaliese gasped, a strange look flashed across her face, but was gone so quickly, Cory didn't have time to understand it. "You talk!"

Cory gave a slight smile. She wasn't sure if she liked it when people who knew her as mute realized she could talk. It was disconcerting and seemed to emphasize her peculiarity. She felt more at ease talking with people who had never known her as unspeaking.

Annaliese didn't seem to notice Cory's hesitancy. "You look awesome girl. Hey, I missed you." Without pausing, she pulled Cory into a bear hug. Cory's nerves about talking melted instantly.

"You too. I am so glad you are here, but how come you are here? What happened?"

Annaliese pulled back, her face falling. "It's a long story." She sighed before pausing and then adding, "I guess it isn't really. It was all so fast, and everything changed. I still can't believe it. I'll tell you later, it isn't really a school lobby discussion."

Cory quickly thought through her options. She didn't need art class and she didn't think Mr. Smythe would mind her missing class. He would probably mark her as absent, but since she didn't plan on making skipping a habit, she didn't think she'd get in trouble for missing just this once. In the end, her desire to see Annaliese along with her dread of talking to Damian swayed her decision about leaving school in the middle of the day.

"Well, good thing we don't need to stay at school. My art teacher won't mind that I am gone." For some reason, she couldn't explain, she tacked on, "He won't mark me absent either. I know a coffee shop close by. We can go talk." Cory took her friend's arm in hers and led her out of the school.

CHAPTER 32

Cory and Annaliese walked together toward the coffee shop chatting about their surprise at ending up at the same school.

"Where are the boys?" Cory finally asked.

Annaliese's face fell. She looked torn. "I don't know." She finally said. "I am pretty sure they are together, or they will be eventually. They try to keep siblings together, but it sometimes takes a while to find the right placement. I wanted to stay with them, but we all knew that wasn't going to happen. Nobody is going to take in three foster kids all at once when they aren't even related."

"Why did you all have to leave?" Cory asked quietly.

Annaliese stopped in the middle of the sidewalk. She was frozen for a minute before she said, "Ms. Grout. She, she died."

"What?" Cory gasped. "How?"

"They say she died in her sleep. I didn't know. I would have tried to get her help, but I didn't know." Annaliese looked heartbroken. Her expression struck Cory as strange; she didn't think Annaliese was that attached to her foster mother, but, she rationalized, Annaliese had lived there much longer than she did. She probably did form an attachment to the old woman.

"Annaliese, what happened?" Cory stood in front of Annaliese putting her hands on her shoulders and looking directly in her eyes. Cory had an inexplicably bad feeling about what happened to Ms. Grout.

Annaliese gulped and took a breath before explaining. "I got up in the morning and Ms. Grout wasn't in the living room. I didn't think anything of it. We were never allowed in her room, so I didn't check there. The boys and I, we just got ready for school and we left. She wasn't around that night either. I started to get a little worried, but not enough to check. By the next morning, when we still hadn't seen her, I knew something was up. I knocked on her door, but of course, she didn't answer. I opened it just a crack, to peek in. She, she..." Her voice trailed off.

Cory stood in silent encouragement for Annaliese to finish her story.

"She was dead."

Cory gasped. "What?"

"Yeah, she probably died that first night, but I don't know, maybe if I would have checked that first morning, maybe I could have gotten her some help and she wouldn't be dead." Annaliese covered her face and let out a single sob.

Cory gave her a sympathetic hug. Ms. Grout wasn't in the best health, but it was surprising that she died so suddenly.

They finished their walk to the coffee shop without saying much. To Cory, Annaliese seemed a little lost. They ordered vanilla steamers and had a seat at the same back table that Cory sat at on Saturday.

"I don't like feeling this way, Cory."

"Like what?"

"Like I should have done something. Maybe it didn't have to be like this. I mean I am happy. I feel like I am where I am supposed to be. I am here with you and I like my new placement." She smiled at Cory, "but I feel bad about Mrs. Gout. I feel like this is somehow my fault." She reached her hand to her eyes to dab at tears Cory couldn't see.

Cory started to speak, but Annaliese stopped her by shaking her head and holding up her hand. "I don't know why. I know in my head it isn't my fault. It's just that I can't help the way I feel."

Saying nothing, Cory reached across the table to give Annaliese's hand a squeeze. She wanted to say something comforting, but she couldn't find the right words. She let her silence speak for her instead.

"I have been at the Grout's the longest. She was totally unbalanced, a definite cheapskate, and basically used us all for manual labor, but I knew how to deal with her, you know?"

Cory gave her a tightlipped smile and held back a giggle of agreement. To say Annaliese knew how to deal with her was an understatement.

"Okay, so when I talk about her, she kind of sucked right? But, it was home. I was doing alright there. I just worry about what will happen next. I feel out of control, but also right somehow, like maybe it was fate."

Cory wanted to reassure her, but she knew how tenuous her placement could be. She didn't want to give false reassurance.

"Where are you staying now?"

"I am with a couple of do-gooders with grown kids out of the house. It seems okay. At least I think it will work out. I mean I only have a year and a half. I am just going to keep my head down and ride out my time."

"Yeah, I get that." Cory fully understood how plans depended on birthdays.

"What's going on with you? You look good and you talk now too." A gleam flashed so quickly in Annaliese's eyes Cory thought she imagined it. "What's up with that? Did you always talk and just didn't when you were with us?" Her face was alight with curiosity.

Cory laughed. "No, it's not like that. I just started up again. It has been kind of hard, but I have been working on it since I got here. I, uh, quit talking before, when I was eight."

"Dang, girl." Annaliese whistled.

"I know."

"So, you're going with the alternative sexy instead of foot in the grave, zombie look?" Annaliese asked.

Cory laughed. She hadn't thought that much about it. "Other than when I helped at a wedding the other day, this is new. I was trying to go for powerful." She cocked what would have been an eyebrow and tried to look imposing.

"Powerful. Um, I am not sure that is the vibe I am getting, but okay."

They laughed, but then Cory started to feel somewhat dismal. She shook her head. "I kind of screwed up and I felt like if I looked less like myself it would be easier to not feel as anxious."

"I am not sure I am following your logic, but what's going on?" This time Annaliese reached across the table to squeeze Cory's hand.

It took Cory a few minutes to gather her thoughts. Annaliese sipped her drink. "I was sort of seeing this guy. Well, I guess not seeing, but we hung out a few times. Anyway, he asked me to a dance and I thought he liked me, but Saturday I saw him making out with another girl. I told him I didn't want to see him and that I was going to go the dance with someone else. I told him I was going with my boyfriend."

Annaliese sat in utter stillness as Cory covered her eyes to childishly hide her face for a moment before continuing.

"When he asked who, I gave him the name of another guy at the school because I was embarrassed that I lied that I was going to the dance and that I had a boyfriend." Cory sighed before finishing, "the problem is that he is a cute guy, he has a girlfriend, and she found out and confronted me about it. I am sure he knows too. I can't believe I did it. I just can't face either one of them again, ever."

Cory groaned out the end of her story and waited for Annaliese to concur that she was the stupidest person who ever lived, and she should definitely never go back to school. To her surprise, Annaliese started to snicker.

"Girlfriend, seriously, that is your big drama? You have it going on, stupid boy number one shouldn't have bothered sniffing around someone else when he could be with you. Stupid boy number two would probably be thrilled with someone like you. You know what you need to do, you need to walk in the school like you own the place and not even think twice about any of it. Be on the lookout for stupid boy number three. You got me?"

Cory smiled hesitantly at first, and then it grew wider. "Thank you. I think I will do exactly that. I am so glad you're here."

Annaliese looked down at her drink, her expression somewhat morose.

"Hey," Cory said, understanding her look and forgetting her desire to avoid possibly bogus comfort, "you have found a good place. You are going to be happy at your new home and you are going to find your way, okay?"

Annaliese gave her an appraising look that lasted long enough for Cory to begin to feel uncomfortable.

"Should we make our way back to school? I think we can make it back for the last class." Cory smiled impishly.

"You can. I don't even have class today. I just have to call for my ride home." She huffed a breath onto her fingernails and pretended to buff them against her shirt.

Cory threw a balled-up napkin at her head.

"Ooh, you know what we could do? We could go back to school and you could point out those two guys you're crushin' on."

"I am not crushing on anyone." Cory said indignantly, "but I will point them out. They are both totally cute."

They giggled on their way back to school. Cory's mood was soaring.

Annaliese's foster mom texted that she'd be in front of the school waiting for her in fifteen minutes.

Since they had the time, Annaliese walked with Cory to her locker. She had a couple minutes before the bell rang and the halls would start to swell with people. As anticipated, Cory was busy swirling her lock, trying to get the right combination when the bell rang.

"Ugh," she huffed when the lock didn't open. "I hate it when I don't get it right."

Annaliese smiled, her attention shifting to her new classmates roaming through the hall.

Cory's lock clicked and released just before a strong arm grabbed her around the waist. She was enveloped in a hug from behind and assaulted with a clean, masculine smell. Whoever was hugging her leaned down and kissed her once one the cheek and once again under her left ear.

Cory and Annaliese's expressions were mirror images reflecting total surprise. Their eyes were wide while their mouths hung open in shock.

"Hey, Cory, sorry I can't talk right now. I have to run to get to the gym. I'll call you tonight, alright?" Jaxson's words were rushed. He was halfway down the hall before Cory could pull herself together enough to nod.

"So, was that stupid boy number one or number two?" Annaliese asked in a whisper as breathless as if she were the one who had been kissed.

CHAPTER 33

Cory walked home in a daze. She was convinced Jaxson was acting out an elaborate hoax. He obviously heard that she had told Damian they were dating and was somehow making fun of her, but she didn't understand. Nobody besides Annaliese was there to see him kiss her in the hall.

Maybe he was trying to play a joke on Damian, but it didn't make sense. She wondered if he was playing some sort of joke on her with Damian. Maybe they were trying to work together to mess with her. Maybe they thought it would be funny to lead her on somehow. It was stupid, but the most likely option she could come up with.

She stifled a growl of frustration and thought about Annaliese's words to act like she owned the place. She would be on the lookout for boy number three.

She could do that.

She felt stronger now that Annaliese went to her school. She had a real friend and confidante.

She tried to stop thinking of Jaxson. It still bothered her that she didn't understand why he kissed her in the hallway. It seemed so out of character.

Although the truth was, she hadn't minded. Jaxson was really good looking. So, what if it was just a joke? She liked having his attention on her. She could pretend he was her boyfriend, couldn't she?

She heard Miranda banging around in the kitchen when she walked in the door.

She didn't bother calling out, instead, she quietly made her way to her aunt.

"Oh, Cory!" She screeched. "You startled me. I ..." She twisted her wrist to look down at her watch, "oh, I guess I lost track of time. I wasn't expecting you home yet."

Cory smiled. "Sorry about that. I will work on being louder."

Miranda laughed. "I guess you will need to work on that. You've been so quiet for so long."

Her smile faded from her lips, "Cory, I hate to spring this on you, but now that you are speaking, I need you to talk to someone."

"What? Who?" Cory asked.

"I need you to talk to Lilah. She needs to explain a few things about our family."

"What? Why can't you?" Confusion colored her tone.

"It isn't my place to talk to you. I don't have all the information, but it needs to be done."

"But why Lilah?" Cory couldn't keep the whine out of her voice.

"She is the best one right now. You need to talk with her and you need to know."

"Know what?" Cory asked.

Miranda pursed her lips but didn't answer.

"Okay, fine," Cory said giving in. "When do you want me to talk with her?"

"She's going to come over tonight, after dinner."

"What? Tonight? I wanted to get some painting in tonight. I haven't done anything all day." She knew she sounded unreasonable, but she couldn't help it. She didn't want to talk to Lilah. She needed time for her art. She hadn't had any all day, there was even a tiny part that regretted skipping art class to spend time with Annaliese that afternoon.

"She won't be here long, and you really need to talk with her." Her tone was unyielding. Cory decided she wasn't going to win the argument and she might as well get it over with.

As promised, as soon as they were done washing the dishes and wiping down the kitchen table, the doorbell rang.

"I'll get it." Miranda said before walking out of the room. Cory followed a few steps behind her.

Lilah stood in the living room wearing a light blue cardigan over a cream-colored t-shirt, and a pair of faded skinny jeans. Her presence commanded attention. She didn't wait for an invitation before taking a seat on the couch in the living room.

Awkwardly, Miranda pointed toward her bedroom and said, "I just should, um, go to my room."

Cory glared at her. Why did she have to invite Lilah over and then not even stay when she got there? It seemed uncharacteristically sneaky and underhanded for her aunt.

"I knew you were talking," Lilah said bluntly.

Cory had no response. She didn't know what business it was of Lilah's if she talked or not.

They sat studying each other for a moment.

"Let's get this out in the open; I don't like you," Lilah said decisively as she stared across the room to Cory, disgust evident in her eye.

Cory huffed but didn't say anything as she crossed to the recliner and had a seat.

"Okay, great. The feeling is mutual," She finally responded, trying to make her voice sound board and unaffected. Why did Lilah have it out for her anyway? It wasn't like they knew anything about each other.

Lilah continued as if Cory hadn't said anything. "You should know why I don't like you."

"Does it matter?" Cory snapped.

"It does." Lilah leaned across the table to get closer to Cory. "I don't like you because you shouldn't be here." She spoke slowly, emphasizing each of her words.

"It isn't like I want to be here talking to you either." Cory spat. "Miranda said I had to talk to you. Here I am. If you don't have anything to say, then fine. Either take it up with Miranda, or you can leave."

Lilah's eye's narrowed. "No. It isn't that you shouldn't be here in this house." She made a sweeping motion around the room with her hands. "What I mean is that you shouldn't be here at all. As in on this Earth. You should be dead. Eight years ago, you should have died. But you didn't."

Cory felt the breath leave her body. She was completely shocked.

"I do need to talk to you. There are some things you need to know." Lilah lowered her voice and continued. "Your mother. She kept you alive for selfish reasons. What she did goes against everything. It goes against the rules. It puts us all at risk."

"What are you talking about? My mother, rules, I have no idea what you mean?" Cory's mind was reeling. She wanted nothing more than to escape from this conversation.

"I forget that you know nothing about our heritage." Lilah sneered. "I will start from the beginning."

Her tone was condescending, Cory wondered for the first time in her life what it would like to slap someone across the face.

"We come from a long line of gifted individuals. It has been passed down from mothers to daughters for eons. Over the millennia, we have been known as many things. We have been called everything. Sometimes we were known as mystics, sometimes seers, enchantresses, or sorcerers. Often, we were called witches. But none of the names were quite right. We prefer gifted. We have been gifted as caretakers of fey magic.

"Of course," she continued as if what she said made complete sense, "we haven't always been as secretive as we are today. In times when we have been well-known, we were sought after and revered for our talents. You can imagine how valuable we would be in certain situations. We make wars change their course. We make people do what we say. Our family gifts can and have changed the course of history over and over again. If we say something happened, then it did. We always get what we want."

Her beautiful eyes clouded over, "We had everything. We could create the outcomes we wanted with only a word. Even though it never seemed necessary to our ancestors, we were given protectors, individuals made to help, care for, and shield us from our enemies. As I said, they weren't needed. But then one day another group, something like a family, emerged that wanted us for our gifts. They also had a supernatural power but it was different from ours. They sought to control us and could leech some of our power onto themselves, leaving our gifted ancestors as insubstantial as shadows. As a family, we were hunted to near extinction."

Cory sat wide-eyed, listening in earnest.

"While our losses were devastating, it turned out to be the best thing possible for those who remained." Lilah's spine straightened with pride. "We never forgot our history. We never forgot what was done to us. We never forgot what they were capable of."

"To save ourselves and our way of life, we ran, and we hid. We became secretive and never let anyone find out about us again. We will never again be persecuted the way we once were. We all keep together and we keep the family secret."

Cory sat dumbstruck, completely forgetting her dislike for Lilah. She was fascinated and wanted to know more.

In a quiet voice, she managed to squeak out, "what does this have to do with me?"

"You are one of us. You have to abide by the rules to keep us all safe, but you don't know any of them." She looked haunted.

"Your mother interfered with what was supposed to happen. Then she kept you removed and isolated. She wanted to protect you, but in her actions, she has threatened to disrupt all of our lives."

Cory was more confused than ever. "I don't understand."

"First of all, not all of us have the ability to create truths, but all of us who do share teal colored eyes."

"Miranda," Cory whispered, thinking of her aunt's eyes.

"No." Lilah snapped. "Not Miranda. She has no power even though she has the right eye color. We thought the same was true of your mother. However, that was found to be false. She did have the power."

"Rules for our kind are to never expose our secret, never change life or death outcomes, and there must be the smallest grain of truth to embellish as we see fit. We cannot lie. If we try, our words become truth. It is a part of the fairy in us. Fairies do not lie.

"Nobody, including your mother, thought she had the gift. Because of this, she was not closely monitored. That was a mistake.

"She chose to separate from the family when she married your father. Nonna said he was a jealous and possessive man.

"Years later, he took you to hurt her. You were murdered. You were supposed to die from either the smoke inhalation or your stab wounds."

She spoke in such a matter of fact tone it forced

her to think about things she tried hard to forget. Cory shivered as she tried to quickly suppress the flood of memories flashing through her mind.

"You were carried from the house. You should have died from your wounds alone. There was no way you could have survived your injuries plus the damage from the smoke. The paramedics were only with you long enough to pronounce you dead before they left you to search for survivors."

Cory wondered how and why Lilah knew so much about her history.

Lilah looked thoughtfully at Cory before she continued, "We don't know exactly how it happened. Maybe your mother had a surge of power that caused her to change your fate. Or perhaps, the paramedics missed the faintest sign of life. There must have been something. Otherwise, even with a power surge, she wouldn't have been able to keep you alive. There always has to be a grain of truth."

"She is the one that changed your outcome. She said that you had been hurt badly, but that you lived. It was a lie she wanted to believe. I don't know if she meant to revise the truth or if she was in delusional grief, but at the moment the words left her lips, someone heard you gasp. They hurried to work on you. After you were stabilized, they rushed you to the hospital.

"They saved you, but you should have died. She went against the rules. All of them. It was the only time we know of that she used her gift, but it was powerful and unexpected.

"You lived, but your recovery was intense. She kept you isolated from us, we wanted to know more about you. We made sure she kept us informed about your progress. We weren't going to let the two of you go unmonitored. We were not going to make the same mistake a second time. We watched you closely for signs of the gift"

"But then you didn't talk. We wondered if you were unable to talk. We thought it might have been the result of you being brought back from the dead. Maybe it was your curse for being something that shouldn't exist."

Cory shook her head as if to clear the words from her mind, Lilah's story seemed so implausible. A family heritage built on magic couldn't be real but something about it seemed to resonate with her. She had often thought she should have been dead, killed by her own father. Now at least she knew the reason for her existence. She wanted to think more about it, but she couldn't. At least not yet. She needed Lilah to stop talking. She hated the way Lilah spoke of her mother and made it seem like her mother's love was less important than keeping a family secret. Her mother had gone against the rules in an effort to keep her alive. Nobody could fault a mother for keeping a child alive.

But it did make intuitive sense not to interfere with life and death. She felt her blood run cold as her mind flashed on Annaliese and Mrs. Grout. Had she interfered by inadvertently causing Ms. Grout's death when she told Tabby Annaliese was coming to her school? It was too much of a coincidence. She hadn't known anything about her ability when it happened, but would she be held responsible for it anyway? She wanted to ask, but she wouldn't ask Lilah. She didn't dare. She couldn't draw attention to her possible deeds.

Without recognizing Cory's inner turmoil, Lilah continued. "Nobody knew if you were gifted or not. The gift usually manifests itself with puberty. Since you didn't speak, it didn't really matter if you were or weren't. You mother wanted to keep you from finding out about the family. She wanted to keep you separate from us. She made sure you wanted for nothing. She made sure you had no need to speak. By keeping you mute, she kept us from getting too close.

"When she died, and Miranda took you in, you were brought back to the fold. By birth, you are a part of the family, but because you were silent, we decided not to tell you our secrets. We weren't going to inform you of anything unless you showed signs of having the ability."

"You weren't as easy to monitor as we anticipated. We were sure if you ever spoke, it would be to Miranda. If it ever happened, she would let us know, and we could figure out if you had the gift, in a safe environment that wouldn't put anyone in danger.

"That didn't happen. You spoke outside of the family. You said you were dating Jaxson. You lied, and it caused your words to become truth. Who knows what other trouble you've caused. You need to know about your ability and you need to know the rules. I will be the one to teach you."

"Why?" Cory asked. "You said yourself you don't like me. Why would you bother to teach me?"

Lilah's eyes clouded over. At first, Cory thought she wouldn't answer.

"It's my role, Cory. It is my responsibility to guide the family, to make sure our secrets are kept, and the rules are followed. I am the chosen one. The grandmothers chose me when I was young because I was powerful. They taught me everything. Now I must watch and guard. Someday, I will choose another to teach and she will keep the family going."

Cory felt her mind in turmoil and her heart being clenched. She wanted more than anything to talk with her mother. She wanted to know more about what happened that night, how she was saved, and why her mother wanted to keep her from knowing the truth.

Lilah remained silent for several moments before she stood and started to walk gracefully to the door. Her hand reached for the knob, as she twisted it open she added, "Cory until you understand everything, you must only speak the truth. Even after you know about your gift, you must be truthful. Always."

CHAPTER 34

Cory didn't move for several minutes. She hated the way the conversation with Lilah made her feel. She wondered if Lilah had some sort of mental health issue, maybe she needed to go to a special hospital or something. But there was a small part of her wondering how much of what she said was true. Some of what she said felt like it fit. She combed through the events of the past couple weeks, trying to remember exactly what she had said. She needed to think about what she said, what was true, and what happened in the end.

She remembered the lunch in her bag that she never packed. At the time, she thought Miranda did it, but maybe she didn't. She said Annaliese would be transferring to her school and then she did. She told Damian she was going out with Jaxson, and then Jaxson kissed her in the hall at school like they were dating. She knew when she said these things they weren't true. As soon as the words came out of her mouth, she had felt embarrassed for telling such obvious lies. But then they weren't lies in the end. Could it all be a series of unlikely coincidences or was there some truth to her having a gift?

She felt a headache starting to build behind her eyes. She didn't want to think about Lilah or her words. She didn't want to think about what was true or what wasn't. She needed a break from thinking

She made her way up to her room. Trying to block Lilah's words from her brain.

She turned on the water in the shower and stripped out of her clothes. She let it get as hot as she could stand before stepping into the spray.

Lilah's words kept infiltrating her thoughts. She heard the mantra "gifted, you shouldn't be here, she kept you here, she broke the rules" repeated over and over again in her mind.

Cory felt the tears mix with the water. What Lilah had said was crazy. She couldn't believe it was true, but it made sense, somewhat. She always thought she should have died that night. Her mother always said she was lucky to have lived, but she never believed that. She never felt worthy enough to survive. It was part of the reason she didn't speak.

She remembered that day in vivid detail. Her father picked her up from school. That wasn't a normal occurrence. He drove her to that house in his grey pick-up truck with black interior. She had been cold. She didn't have a jacket and the air conditioner was blowing at full blast, but he wouldn't turn it down. She was shivering. He was sweating. She watched it roll down the side of his face. He was ranting about her mother, saying horrible things about her; things that a child should never have to hear about anyone, especially their mother. She was scared, but it was an unnamed fear. She was scared, but even then, she couldn't imagine him hurting her.

As they drove, she noticed the maniacal gleam in his eye as he muttered about how he would show her. She thought he had forgotten that she was in the truck with him. He was completely fixated on her mother. She heard enough of his plan to know he wanted to try to hurt her mother as deeply as he could because she had the audacity to try to live and be happy without him. In her young mind, she couldn't fathom his intentions. At that time, she didn't know what it meant to be out of your mind crazy.

"I'll show her," she remembered him muttering over and over again. "I will take everything from her. She will be nothing."

When he stopped the car in the driveway, he threw the truck in park, and practically ran into the house without looking back. She quietly followed him and shut the door behind her. Then she sat on the couch in the living room to watch his flailing movements and listen to his rambling words. She was only eight years old, but she would never forget the way the cheap velvet on the couch felt against her legs as she squeezed an old, musty smelling pillow to her chest trying to comfort herself like a small child clutching a beloved teddy bear.

The longer she sat, the more her stomach seemed to tie itself in knots. She remembered having trouble swallowing. It felt like a ball was growing in her throat. She didn't dare utter a word to the man she called daddy. She waited for him to calm down. At that point, she still had no suspicion that he would try to hurt her. She was scared for him. He was acting strange, but she had no instinct to try to run or to hide. He was her dad. At that moment, if anyone asked, she would have said he would never hurt her.

She remembered hearing his heavy boots on the floor. From where she sat she couldn't see him, but she knew he was in the kitchen. Looking back, she realized that must have been when he got the knife. It was a cheap paring knife with a flimsy blade and an orange handle. She would never forget that knife.

When he came back into the room, he was yelling words she didn't understand. His eyes were glazed. She didn't recognize him as her dad. His face was contorted with rage. Then, in a flash, he began to hurt her. He grabbed her around the waist with one hand and pulled her off the couch, holding her off the ground so her small back was against his chest. He began to stab her with the knife. She remembered feeling equal parts shock, pain, and warmth as her blood pulsed out of her. Later, one of her doctors told her mother when they thought she was asleep how the flimsy knife blade probably saved her life. It hadn't gone directly into a vital organ; the angle of the blade was deflected by her bone changing one of the lethal strikes into a superficial cut. In her haze, she remembered wondering why her dad hadn't chosen a more substantial knife. Maybe there had been a part of him that knew what was going on and didn't want to hurt her.

When he stopped, he threw her to the ground. Looking back, she realized he must have stopped because he was convinced she was dead. It was hard for her to remember things clearly after being thrown to the floor. She remembered the smell of the gasoline and the sloshing sound it made as he splashed it against the house. Then she heard the boom of a gunshot.

After the gunshot, she wasn't scared anymore. She felt cold and detached, but there was no pain. She wanted to move, but she couldn't. She saw flashing lights from the firetruck and ambulance from where she lay. She watched the lights dance in circles around the room. She remembered thinking they were pretty. They reminded her of a television show she had seen about a teenage dance party.

She smelled the smoke and wanted to get outside, but she couldn't. Her body would not obey her mind telling her to move. She felt herself fading away, like she was drifting in a warm ocean. She remembered a sense of peace settled over her.

A fireman seemed to appear out of nowhere. He was dressed like an astronaut in all his gear. He picked her up and carried her little body outside. She felt safe. She knew she'd be okay. She remembered whispering to the man who couldn't hear her through the chaos and his protective gear, "I'm okay. You saved me. I am going to make it and I will go home with my mom when I get better."

Did her whispered words save her life because of a family gift? It was possible and, according to Lilah, against a set of rules she never knew existed.

Her memories became even hazier and more disjointed after that. She remembered shouting all around her. There was someone pounding on her chest, but in her memories, she couldn't tell if that happened outside the house or in the hospital. Or maybe both.

Then everything was dark for a long time.

And then her mother was there. Sitting beside her in a cold white room that smelled like cleaning supplies. She remembered her mom's head leaning on her bed rail, her body twisted awkwardly so she could be close and hold her hand.

Cory shut off the water in the shower and tried to push the memories back into her subconscious. She didn't want to remember. She didn't want to think about her recovery and her struggles. Her stomach lurched as she threw back the shower curtain and stumbled out of the surround before vomiting her stomach contents into the toilet.

She couldn't let the memories come bubbling to the surface. They did nothing good for her. She couldn't think of him. It was too difficult to try to reconcile the dad she loved with the monster who tried to kill her just to spite her mother. She wasn't ready to think of her mom. Losing her was still too recent. She couldn't bear thinking about never seeing her again.

She wrapped her hair in a towel and another around her body. Then splashed cold water on her face, brushed her teeth, and dried the bathroom floor.

Part of her felt like taking another shower. The one she had taken didn't do anything to help her relax. She wished more than anything she could talk to her mom. She had often wished she had talked to her about her father, about that day, and now, she wished she could talk to her about their family and their secret.

Then it hit her.

Her mother's journal. She didn't have the luxury of worrying about invading privacy. She needed answers and maybe the journal was the key.

She crept to her dresser, opened the bottom drawer and pushed aside the clothes she had piled on top of them.

She had carefully hidden them when she got home. Instinctively she hadn't wanted to read them. It felt wrong somehow. Plus, she was afraid of what reading her mother's thoughts might stir within her.

She took a deep breath and pulled them to her chest. She shifted her weight so her back was leaning against the drawers. She had to know. She had to make herself read them.

Her mother had started writing in them when Cory was unconscious in the hospital. It hurt to read how scared her mother was about what had happened. Surprisingly, she didn't seem to hate her father. She seemed, not to forgive his actions, but to forgive him so she could move on. Idly, she wondered if she would have been able to forgive if the roles were reversed.

Cory traced the blurry words with her fingertips. Her mother must have been crying when she wrote about her fears. It must have been her tears that smeared the ink. Her mother had intended to take her own life if Cory had died. Cory felt her heart was cracking for her mother's pain. She had been in a coma for so long, her condition tenuous, and her mother had to endure through it all.

By the end of the first journal, her mother wrote about Cory getting stronger. The entries became more optimistic. The last entry in the first journal was about Cory opening her eyes for the first time. Hope, love, and optimism were reflected in her mother's writing.

Cory smiled to herself as she closed the first journal and opened the second.

There had been a passage of time between the first journal and the second. According to the journal, she had been transferred to the rehabilitation hospital by that time. The tone of the entries had changed. Her mother was worried. She was no longer afraid that Cory wouldn't make it. She was afraid that the family would find out.

There was a single cryptic entry where her mother reflected on true power. She wrote that she would be lost without Cory and that she would always protect her. Cory read the entry over and over trying to make it make sense.

I grew up knowing about the gift. I remember the grandmothers watching Miranda and me to see if we had it. When they were sure we didn't, it was like nobody cared about us anymore. We went from being prized daughters to wastes of space. We meant nothing to any of them. All for a secret that forces us to live in isolation. I will never put my daughter through that. Why would I want a gift I couldn't use?

I couldn't wait to get as far away from them as possible. I wanted nothing more to do with any of them. I got away from them as soon as I had the chance.

I was thrilled when I got pregnant. I wanted to be a mother. Then I had her, my beautiful daughter. I was heartbroken the first time she opened her eyes to look at me and I saw the color, that beautiful teal color. I cried because I never wanted her to be trapped in the family and exposed to risk. Teal eyes made the risk a possibility. I made a promise that I would protect her from everyone for all of my days.

Right now, I feel like I am entering a nightmare. I am the only one who knows none of it was me. I didn't keep Cory alive. I know for sure I don't have the power. What I don't know is if it was Cory herself who has the gift and used it to save her own life or if I owe her life to an actual miracle.

At least, for now, she isn't talking. I can breathe for the moment and not worry. Nobody in the family will be interested in her if she isn't speaking. Is it horrible of me that I am glad she won't talk or that I hope she stays that way for a while? All I want is for my baby girl to be safe. It would be so much easier if she never spoke a single word for the rest of her life. It would keep them from getting too close. I can't let them become interested in her. What would it mean if she had the gift now? She is far too young. I can't let anything happen to her. I came so close to losing her. I can't go through that pain again, ever.

I will protect my baby at any cost. I wonder if I can keep her from speaking? Maybe if I took care of everything she could possibly need, she wouldn't have a reason to speak again. That way, she could be safe from all the forces that would conspire against her if she had the gift.

For several minutes, Cory was sat frozen. Her mother had kept her from speaking on purpose, although she didn't quite understand how or why. She wanted to be angry at her mom for helping to keep her from speaking, but she couldn't. Her mom may have set her up for silence, but she was the one who made the decision not to talk.

She desperately wanted to know more, but there were no other entries in the journal. She was frustrated at the lack of details. She wondered if she could be in danger now that she was talking, and the family knew. She wasn't completely convinced the family gift was real and like her mother, she wasn't sure she actually had it.

She felt a surge of anger as she wondered why hadn't her mother ever confided in her. Shouldn't she have been told the family secret? Was her mother really trying to protect her? Or could they all be delusional? Maybe it was a genetic mental health issue they all shared.

She had to stop thinking. She was going to make herself crazy for real.

She pressed her palms to her eyes and stretched her legs out in front of her. It was getting late and she told herself she needed to go to bed, but she knew sleep was never going to happen. She needed to let her mind go. She shoved the journal under her pillow and decided to paint.

She was frustrated to find several tubes of paint empty. Irritated, she pushed her paints aside and dug out her pastels. They were used to the point of nubs. Her large paper book had no blank pages. It was disturbing to be out of so many supplies all at once. She needed money for more and she still hadn't figured out her job situation.

Then a thought occurred to her.

Lilah did tell her how important it was for her to always tell the truth, but she needed art supplies and she needed proof. Once she knew for sure if there was a family gift, she could figure out what to do next.

She would tell one lie, something obviously untrue and unknown by anyone else. If her lie became true, she would consider Lilah's story possible. Since she needed art supplies anyway, she had to think of a test that could work out as a way for her to get art supplies at the same time. Assuming the whole gift thing was real.

She sat on her bed with her eyes closed. Finally, a slow smile spread across her face as she thought about her options.

Once her plan solidified, she quietly walked to Miranda's room. She knocked gently on the door and stood waiting until Miranda looked up.

She was sitting up in bed, glasses perched on the end of her nose, reading one of her favorite romance novels. "Cory, what's up?" She asked, wearily. Cory glanced at the clock and wished she had waited until morning to set her plan in motion, but it was too late.

"Miranda, I wanted to let you know that I have been working on getting back into modeling again." She paused feeling a little ridiculous. "I have a job booked for Saturday afternoon, a calendar shoot. I thought you should know."

Cory looked directly at Miranda waiting for something to happen. Miranda looked confused for the briefest moment before understanding crossed her features.

"Oh, right, yes. I got an email from Carl Beacham at Beacham Photography. They did the wedding that you helped at the other day. I guess Carl snapped a picture of you serving and thought you would be perfect for a retro calendar they are doing. He said something about fixing you up to look like a 1950s Barbie doll." Miranda giggled and looked back at her book.

Cory didn't know what to say. She remembered her picture being snapped at the wedding, but that was it.

"Right, Beacham Photography, that's right. He

sent you the email. He gave you all the information we need. You have the directions and you don't have a wedding scheduled. Do you think you can give me a ride? It starts at 1 o'clock."

"Yes, the email did say 1 o'clock. I'd love to give you a ride. I was hoping you'd let me stay and watch. I've never seen an actual calendar shoot before. I'd love to see you in action."

Miranda gazed indulgently at her while Cory tried to smile, but only managed a sick looking grimace. Maybe she chose the wrong test. This was too easy. There was a photographer at the wedding who took her picture. Maybe her test wasn't good enough. Sure, she lied and told Miranda she was going to model, but her test was too plausible. She had been a model as a child. A photographer did take her picture recently. Maybe he had sent Miranda and email. Was it so far-fetched that the same photographer would ask her to do some modeling now?

She would see what happened on Saturday, but she needed more of a test to know for sure. Right now, everything felt too coincidental.

She had to think of some way to prove she had some sort of supernatural gift or not. If she did have some kind of power, she would need to really know what it could do. She couldn't trust the explanations and rules given to her by Lilah.

CHAPTER 35

She reached over to smack the alarm clock sitting on her nightstand and then rolled back over to wait for the snooze alarm to go off. Her brain was slowly starting to adjust to being awake. Her first thought was surprise that she had slept well that night. She didn't think she would, not with all the nonsense Lilah filled her head with before bed.

Cory woke up feeling invigorated, clear-headed, and completely sure that Lilah had an overzealous imagination or a disturbing sense of humor. She wasn't going to be taken in by any of it. She wouldn't let Lilah have that sort of power over her. She could imagine Lilah making fun of her at some future get together for falling for her elaborate, and honestly not very funny joke. She could see her telling the story to a riveted audience laughing at her expense.

She organized her school books frowning at her diminished art supplies. How had she used them up so fast when she hardly ever got a chance to work on her art? She needed to figure out how to make time for art in her new schedule. She'd have to start by asking Miranda when she could expect a check from the catering company. Then she was going to take herself to the art store and stock up.

It was going to be even more difficult to have time for her art if she got a job, even though the purpose of a job was to buy art supplies. She'd have to figure out how to manage. Things were so different now, she felt much more grown up, but where had all her changes gotten her? She started to talk, but talking seemed to open herself to new problems. She needed to take charge of herself. She didn't want to revert to the old

Cory that could do nothing but art, but she wasn't going to open herself up to so much risk anymore either.

She decided the first step was to limit her talking to Miranda, Annaliese, and Jacob. Then, she was going to find a job and she was going to graduate from high school. That was it. She wasn't going to involve herself with Lilah, Damian, or Jaxson. They were going to get the Cory Fall silent treatment and nobody was better at silence than her.

Having made her decisions, she felt good that morning. She brushed her hair smooth before braiding it into a thick side braid, she added black cat eye wings to her eyes, and several silver necklaces and bracelets before deciding she might need to shop for a few colorful pieces of clothing to add to her wardrobe. After all, she was reinventing herself. She made a mental note to buy herself something purple once she had some cash.

As she walked to school, she tried to figure out how Miranda played into Lilah's joke or whatever it was since it wasn't actually funny. It didn't make sense why Miranda would invite Lilah over to give her the opportunity to talk to her about a family secret where lies become true. Then Miranda went along with her own farfetched story about a modeling job over the weekend.

The weird thing was, she hadn't sensed any deception on her aunt's face when they talked about the wedding photographer or calendar shoots. Shouldn't there have been something to indicate Miranda knew what was really going on? Was Miranda that good a liar? Any why?

It just didn't make sense.

"Hey beautiful," she heard yelled to her from across the street. She turned toward the sound to see

Jaxson running toward her. He was tall and graceful as he loped in her direction in his usual black skinny jeans and a well-worn t-shirt that she thought had an image of David Bowie on it, but it was so well-worn she couldn't be sure.

She smiled in spite of herself. She could let this little joke play out a little while longer. She would much rather spend time looking at Jaxson than Lilah.

"Hi, Jaxson." She said forgetting that only an hour before she vowed not to talk to him.

"Hi there." He responded pulling her into a quick hug.

He started to walk toward the school with Cory, his steps quickly adjusting to match her stride.

"So, what did you want to do tonight?" He asked.

"I didn't realize we had plans." She said confused.

"Well, we didn't, but I was hoping to spend some time with my girl." He gave her a flirtatious look, quickly took a hold of her elbow, and then slid his hand down her forearm, to grasp her hand.

She looked down at their joined hands. It seemed so natural. He didn't hesitate at all taking her hand. It was like he already knew she wouldn't mind. It was like he had, like they had, done it before.

"Your girl? Jaxson, please tell me what's going on?" She begged.

His brows scrunched together as he looked at her with confusion. "You can be so strange Cory." He said with a smirk.

"No, really, I am confused. We have hardly talked to one another. We haven't been on a date, but you are holding my hand and calling me your girl." She noticed they hadn't stopped holding hands.

He looked confused again. He ran his free hand through his hair and looked thoughtfully at her.

"Well, I ... I am not sure, but I am supposed to be

here, and you are my girlfriend." He seemed confident of that fact, even though it didn't make sense.

"I don't understand, Jaxson. What do you mean you are supposed to be here? Besides you were seeing Lilah. When did I become your girlfriend?" She was practically begging for answers.

"I was never seeing Lilah. We have only ever been friends. She wanted more, but I never did. I remember being drawn to you that day in the art store. I tried to talk to you, but you were gone so fast. I thought I'd lost my chance. Then I saw you in the cafeteria. I couldn't believe you transferred here. I was surprised, happy, but surprised. The rest, I am not sure. Is it weird that I don't remember? Everything was so clear but then, I don't remember. It is all fuzzy, but I know without a doubt that we are together. What's going on?" He looked like he was in pain.

"So, if I am your girlfriend, we must have gone on a date. Do you remember asking me on a date? Do you remember our first real kiss?" Cory was speaking rapidly. She didn't have the sense that he was participating in a prank. She felt, without a doubt, he was telling the truth at least as he knew it. He really did think of her as his girlfriend, but, like her, he didn't have any recollection how they had gotten to that point.

He took a hold of her shoulders and pulled her close to him. He licked his bottom lip and staring directly into her eyes leaned down to kiss her. His lips felt soft and warm. The kiss was sweet and then deepened.

They held on for several moments before he straightened up. This time he said with surety, "that was our first kiss and you are my girlfriend."

Cory felt breathless and had no desire to question

or argue as they exchanged a shy smile.

They walked hand in hand toward the school when Jaxson asked, "I just remembered, I told the guys we could have band practice at my house tonight. How about you come with me?"

She suppressed the urge to giggle. He looked so nervously childlike. "Yeah, okay, that sounds good. I'd like that."

Jaxson's answering smile was brilliant.

.

CHAPTER 36

Surprisingly the day passed quickly. Cory ate with Jaxson at lunch, she kept an eye out for Annaliese and was a little bummed that she never found her. On the plus side, she never saw Lilah either. She supposed it balanced out in the end.

She expected some sort of confrontation from Damion in art class, but he didn't attempt to talk with her. He stared at her when she first walked into the room, a strange expression on his face. Then it disappeared. He started to draw and seemed to forget she was in the room. He didn't even seem to notice her or anyone else. She felt grateful because she didn't think she had it in her to discuss anything with him, but at the same time it was disconcerting that he didn't even try to apologize for being a jerk.

Then she remembered she told him at the coffee shop that nothing had ever happened between them. Maybe this was nothing. Maybe Damian had no recollection of her. It felt strange. On one hand, she was relieved, but on the other it was unnerving.

She sighed and straightened herself in her chair and looked down at her ruler and blank paper. They were beginning a lesson on linear perspective. They were supposed to draw staircases like M.C. Escher. It wasn't her favorite thing to draw, but intricate disappearing staircases required concentration and she loved how quickly she could lose herself in her work.

When the bell rang to signal the end of her last class, she realized she didn't know where she was supposed to meet Jaxson.

Frowning, she made her way to her locker, hoping

he would be waiting for her.

"Hey there. Are we still on?" His breath was warm against her cheek as he walked up behind her and brushed his lips across her temple.

"I'm looking forward to it." She smiled up at him.

He took her hand, interlacing their fingers together as if they had done it a thousand times, and led her to the parking lot. They stood together next to his car. He explained that it was a classic. A classic faded silver 1984 Cutlass with cushy faded red, well-worn interior. Cory wasn't sure if it was classic or just old.

Jaxson stopped expounding the dubious benefits of his car when a tall thin boy with pale skin, brown eyes, and light blond hair sticking out from under a brown knit beanie stopped in front of them.

"Kade." Jaxson drawled, raising his fist to his friend for a bump.

"Jaxson." The new boy, Kade responded, eyeing Cory. "Who is this?"

"This is my girlfriend, Cory. Cory Fall."

Cory noticed Kade raise an eyebrow and glance sideways toward Jaxson at the word girlfriend, but nothing else was said.

They piled into the car. Almost immediately, Kade started to talk about school, music, video games, basketball, and his shoes. It was as if every thought he had found its way out of his head through his mouth. Jaxson was used to Kade's talking and Cory liked that she didn't have to try to converse. Even though she was now almost normal in her ability to talk, she would never be considered loquacious.

Outside Jaxson's house was a late model, but comparatively new, Honda Civic. Two large boys got out of the car when Jaxson pulled the Cutlass into the driveway.

Jaxson introduced them as Tony and Sean. They seemed nice enough but anxious to start practicing. Soon, they were marching up the stairs to the bonus room where Cory sat in a battered chair in the corner.

She pulled her backpack on top of her lap and rummaged through it. She was annoyed she only had a lined spiral notebook to draw on even though she did have several pencils and one black ballpoint pen.

The band started to warm up as she pulled her legs underneath her in order to better balance her notebook. She leaned her head back in the chair and closed her eyes, trying to brush away feeling like she was intruding on band time. Before long she recognized the song they were playing. Surprised at how good they sounded, her eyes flew open to look at them. She blushed as she realized Jaxson had been staring at her. She returned his subtle smile and then let the music wash over her.

They kept playing. The music was loud but good. She felt her nervousness disappear. She started to draw. Everything fell away. She didn't worry. She didn't think. She just let her hand fly to the beat of the music, her inspiration coming directly from the music to her fingers.

As practice wound down, Cory noticed for the first-time soreness in her wrist from gripping the pencil tightly as her hand raced over the paper. She set the pencil down and stretched her legs out from their crossed position. The pencil rolled off her lap to the ground as she absentmindedly rubbed at her wrist.

Jaxson set his guitar on its stand and sauntered over to where Cory sat.

Cory couldn't hold in her appreciation. "That was incredible. I recognized some of the songs, but not all of them."

His face took on a sheepish expression. "Yeah,

well, we're a cover band mostly, but we do write a lot of our own music."

"I am impressed." She answered.

"Not as impressed as I am, let me see these." He said as he picked up her notebook from her lap. He stared for a moment, and then flipped back a few pages to see her other drawings.

"Cory, they are amazing." He said in his deep husky voice, somewhat horse from his practice.

"Thank you." She whispered. She had to admit, her drawings did look good. Somehow, she had captured the movement of the band in her lines. Her drawings looked alive, almost powerful.

"You know, we have been trying to find someone to design our new logo."

"Really?"

"Yeah, that's what I was doing that day at the art store. I was putting up flyers trying to find someone."

"Oh, yeah, well maybe I can help."

"I am hoping so." He leaned down and brushed his lips across her forehead. She wondered if he could tell her heart was racing at his touch.

He reached a hand out to help her up. "Unfortunately, I should get you home. This was fun. I liked having you here."

"I liked being here." She said looking up at him through her lashes. She wondered if she should simply accept Jaxson as her boyfriend. Maybe it didn't matter how they happened to get together, just that they did. She liked him, but she wanted to make sure what she felt and what he seemed to feel was real. She didn't want to risk breaking her heart on make-believe

CHAPTER 37

On Friday, Cory wanted to see Jaxson but had no idea where he was. He never appeared at her locker and didn't seem to be in the cafeteria at lunch. She didn't want to worry, but she couldn't help thinking that their bizarre relationship had dissolved as quickly as it had formed. She wished she could at least text him to ask where he was, but she didn't want to seem needy and she had forgotten her phone at home on the charger.

By the time school was over, Cory was convinced she imagined her relationship with Jaxson. She wanted nothing more than to go home and forget everything. She hoped he would simply forget they sort of dated. She wished she didn't lie about, accept, or whatever happened for her to get the modeling job tomorrow. Maybe everything could go back the way it was. She could go back to silence and art. It was so much simpler that way.

She wished she could talk to Annaliese. Even if she couldn't tell her everything, it would be nice to talk to her about some things.

She cursed herself again for forgetting her phone at home and then started her walk home.

When she got to her house, she was surprised to see Jaxson sitting with her elderly neighbor, Mr. Bradley, on the front porch.

Mr. Bradley sat bundled in a heavy coat, even though it wasn't cold out. He looked happy with a wide smile and shiny eyes. For some reason, Jaxson looked anxious. He seemed to be having trouble making eye contact with her.

She wondered what they had been talking about.

"Hi." She offered.

"Hello, Cory. Good to see you." Her neighbor said with a bright smile that put her at ease immediately. Even Jaxson seemed to relax slightly.

"I wasn't expecting to see you here," Cory said, turning her attention to Jaxson.

"I wasn't expecting to be here. I just had some things to do and I sort of found myself here. I was hoping you'd be coming home after school. You didn't answer my texts."

She wrinkled her nose and squeezed her eyes shut for the briefest moment. "I know. I left my phone at home. It's been driving me nuts all day."

He smirked. "Glad to know you weren't ignoring me. I was worried."

"No, of course not." She responded. "I really did forget my phone at home. Do you want to come in?"

"Yeah, I'd like that. I can't stay long, but I'd like to see you for at least a little bit."

"Well, I guess that's my cue to get back inside." Her neighbor added, surprising Cory because she had already forgotten he was there.

"Do you need any help?" She asked.

"No, no help needed, my dear. You have a good day, you hear?" He said smiling at her and winked at Jaxson.

Their connection struck Cory as odd. It seemed overly friendly, like they may have known each other before. She supposed it was possible, but it did seem unlikely.

She unlocked her front door and led the way into the house.

She made them both a snack while they talked in the kitchen.

She felt so at ease with Jaxson. She liked talking to him. She felt so normal around him like she didn't

Kelley Connor

need to second guess and overthink every word that came out of her mouth.

"Do you want to come over again tomorrow? The band has practice, but then I thought we could do something. Maybe go to the movies or something."

"I wish I could," she said truthfully, "but I have a photoshoot. I am not sure how long it is going to take."

"Photoshoot, huh?"

"Yeah, for a calendar." There it was again. The lie. Cory felt her cheeks heating up in embarrassment.

"I kind of like that my girlfriend is a model and an artist." He smiled.

"Ugh. I'm not really a model. I am just, I don't know. I just needed some cash for art supplies. It's just a job and that's it."

"Okay, I guess that's what you can call it." He was full on smirking at her now.

"Seriously, I am not a model."

"It seems to me that when your picture is taken for a calendar, you would be a model."

"Ugh." She groaned.

"Why is it so bad to be a model? You're beautiful. You should be a model." His smile was gentle while his eyes smoldered.

She took a deep breath, trying to pull her thoughts together.

"You know, I really like that my girlfriend is a model. My beautiful girlfriend" he leaned forward to kiss behind her ear. She sighed in contentment at the same time his phone rang.

Frustrated, he backed away slightly and pulled his phone out of his pocket.

"Hello." She heard him say before he paused for several seconds.

"Yeah. Oh, right." He paused again.

"Yeah, okay. I'll be there." He glanced at Cory

239

longingly.

"I know. I know. I'll be right over. I promise." He hung up without saying goodbye.

"I'm sorry. I can't stay any longer. I promised Kade before that I would help him."

She held her finger to his lips. "It's okay," she whispered.

"I won't see you Saturday. How about Sunday?" He asked.

"Sunday sounds perfect." She enthused with a smile before walking him to the door.

She felt sorry to see him go but relieved that their relationship was feeling more and more real.

After Jaxson left, she figured she should try to prepare for the photoshoot, but wasn't sure how to go about it. When she was a kid, it was fun. She'd show up and love the attention. She liked getting her hair fixed and putting on fancy clothes. But now that she was almost an adult, would they expect her to do something before she got there?

She decided to glop a deep conditioning treatment into her hair. Then she took off her black nail polish and carefully filed her nails. She figured she would show up tomorrow free of makeup, but she'd have her make up with her in case they wanted her to put it on. After her hair was washed and brushed out, she had done about all she could do to be ready.

She found a book on Miranda's bookshelf she thought she could read. She figured it would be better to read than risk losing herself and her sense of time if she started to work on her art. She wanted to make sure to get a good night's sleep, so she didn't look tired in the morning.

Unfortunately, her plans didn't matter. She tossed and turned all night, anxious about what the day would bring. She was completely irritated with herself for even mentioning a modeling job. If it was her gift that made it happen, then she only had herself to blame. If it was a coincidence she talked about modeling, Miranda might not have remembered the email Mr. Beacham supposedly sent. Again, it was all her fault that she had a modeling job.

She was beyond frustrated with herself.

On Saturday morning, Miranda flitted around doing housework and preparing for the weekend without noticing Cory's black mood.

They ate an early lunch together and then piled into the car to go to the shoot. Cory tried to ignore Miranda's obvious enthusiasm for the outing. She simply wanted to slink away into her room and paint.

Far too quickly, they arrived at the decidedly unglamorous, nearly deserted warehouse where the shoot was being held.

Cory felt slightly cheered that they weren't going anywhere fancy. She hoped the setting would bring Miranda's mood down a few notches. She was bordering on giddy and it was getting on Cory's nerves.

They were greeted by a tall, thin woman who introduced herself as Sammy. Sammy was dressed haphazardly in holey jeans and a tattered tee shirt even though her hair and makeup looked ready for the red carpet.

She ushered Cory to a small room set up for hair and makeup while Miranda left to use the restroom.

Cory sat uncomfortably in the chair in front of Sammy.

Sammy picked up her black comb and looked over Cory's hair with a sneer.

"Well," she scoffed, "it's clear you don't take care of your hair." She made a face like she smelled something bad.

Cory fought the urge to swiftly kick Sammy in the

shin.

Then, fighting a sneaky smile, "Actually, Sammy, I do take care of my hair. My hair is perfect. In fact, it is the best hair you have ever worked with."

Cory wondered if she had laid it on too thick, but Sammy didn't comment. She simply combed.

Cory leaned back and closed her eyes, relishing in her ability. She was starting to believe she did have a gift. It made her wonder what the family had against using it. Certainly, her little embellishments on the truth weren't a big deal.

She heard Miranda enter and start to make small talk with Sammy. Before long, they sounded like old friends. Cory relaxed and let Sammy have her way with her looks.

She studied herself in the mirror once her look was complete. She wore a navy blue sleeveless halter dress with white polka dots, a wide red belt, and a flared skirt. Her black hair, was swooped into a large wave at the front, pinned at the sides, and fell over her right shoulder in large, loose curls. Her face was pale, but not dramatically so, her eyes were intentionally defined with black liner and mascara, her brows drawn on realistically thin, while her lips were highlighted in a red pout. She looked both modern and retro at once. She loved it.

Cory gave Sammy a genuine smile before catching Miranda's teary eyes.

"Cory, I am so proud of you. I just wish your mom was here to see you." Miranda said softly.

"Me too, Miranda. Me too." Cory sighed, her spirit slightly deflated.

"There you are, Miss Fall." Cory sort of recognized the photographer's booming voice as he confidently strode into the room and gave her a peck on the cheek before shaking Miranda's hand and kissing her first on one cheek and then the other.

Cory was photographed again and again in a formal pale peach tulle evening gown, a pair of white capris with a yellow tank top, and a black swimsuit so modest it was sexy.

Cory found herself enjoying the spotlight. She liked posing in different positions. She liked pretending she was a glamorous retro Barbie. She was safe being the girl in front of the camera because it wasn't her. Not really.

As she stood in her swimsuit in front of a bright green screen holding a multi-colored beach ball, Cory could have sworn she saw Annaliese at the far end of the empty warehouse. She was momentarily stunned because she thought they were alone. She tried to crane her neck to get a better look, but Sammy appeared out of nowhere with a soft makeup brush to touch up her nose and forehead. By the time Cory looked up, the warehouse was again empty.

By the end of the shoot, Cory was exhausted. She dressed in her own clothes and half listened to Mr. Beecham discuss the session with Miranda and Sammy. They all seemed happy with the shoot and how the pictures would turn out.

Mr. Beecham promised to get in touch soon. He smiled a toothy smile at Cory and told her she was going to go far with her modeling.

Cory smiled an insincere smile and reminded herself that the session was just a way to get art supplies. As fun as the day was, she had no interest in modeling as a regular job.

On the way to the car, Cory couldn't shake the feeling that she was being watched. She looked around, but everything seemed disserted. She glanced toward Miranda who was still chatting animatedly, obviously unconcerned.

Cory tried to shake off her discontent as they drove to dinner.

In the restaurant, Cory again thought she saw Annaliese. This time she could have sworn she saw her round a corner and disappear through a set of kitchen doors.

Cory shook it off. She reasoned she thought she saw her friend because she hadn't gotten a good night sleep, she had an eventful day, and she was looking forward to talking with Analiese.

Tomorrow, she promised herself, tomorrow, she would call Annaliese and we will go out for coffee.

CHAPTER 38

On Sunday, Cory dug through her boxes, scrounging for supplies. She was frustrated because she actually worked and still didn't have money to spend. Logically she knew the money would come and even if she had a wallet of money there wasn't an art store open; she was just irritated at the moment. Trying to soothe her emotions, she started to sketch on the back of a notebook in blue ballpoint pen.

She was starting to feel herself relax when the doorbell rang.

She pushed away her notebook and trudged toward the door.

She unlocked the deadbolt and swung open the door.

Jaxson stood in the doorframe looking gorgeous, holding his guitar in his hand.

"Hello there." She beamed.

"Hello yourself." He responded before stepping into the living room.

They sat comfortably on the floor leaning against the couch with their legs outstretched talking about their weekend. As the conversation started to wind down into a comfortable silence, Jaxson began to quietly play his guitar and she started sketching in the notebook.

Cory was amazed at how completely content she felt spending time with Jaxson.

By early afternoon, Cory made sandwiches and fruit. They ate picnic style in the living room.

As they finished, Jaxson's phone pinged with a text. She couldn't help but see Lilah's name as he read it.

"Lilah wants to hang out." He said. She bristled.

"Do you really have to see her?" Cory asked uncharitably.

He stared at her for several seconds before responding, "you two got off on the wrong foot."

"That's an understatement." Cory snorted and diverted her eyes.

"No really," Jaxson said earnestly, placing his hand gently on Cory's knee. "Lilah is good people."

"How long have the two of you been friends?" She asked.

He paused to consider her question. "Middle school, I guess." He shrugged his shoulders. "It feels like we've always known each other."

"You two seem close." Cory's voice trailed off. She wanted to ask about their relationship but felt uncomfortable. She wasn't sure she wanted to hear his answer and she didn't like feeling like a jealous, overly possessive girlfriend.

Jaxson smirked as if he knew what she was thinking as he lifted her chin toward him with his index finger. He leaned closer so her eyes had to connect with his. "I can tell you have something else you want to ask me."

Cory hesitated and then said in a rush. "I was wondering if the two of you ever..." Her voice trailed off again as her eyes flashed away from his.

"What?" He asked. "You think Lilah and I...? No. Of course not, nothing has ever happened between us. I mean she asked me out, but I said no. We just aren't like that. I don't feel that way about her."

Cory thought over his words. He didn't feel that way, but did she have feelings for him? But if she did, would it matter?

"Well, what did she want?" Cory asked trying to change the subject.

"When she asked me out?" He looked confused.

Cory rolled her eyes and smiled. "In her text, what did she want?

For some inexplicable reason, he still looked blank.

She couldn't help but laugh. "Just now, when she texted. What did she want?"

She saw comprehension dawn on his features. "Oh yeah," he chuckled. "I already told you. She wanted to hang out." He paused before adding, "with both of us."

The words hung uncomfortably for a moment. Cory felt pretty sure Jaxson didn't have romantic feelings for Lilah, but their relationship was so strange and seemingly artificially fabricated, she felt like she didn't understand the rules. Cory considered the old adage keep your friends close and your enemies closer and thought she should spend time with Lilah. Maybe if she spent time with her, she could learn more about the weirdness that was now part of her life.

Plus, Lilah was friends with Jaxson. Maybe there was some redeeming quality about her.

Maybe.

"You should text her to see if she wants to come over." She blurted before she could talk herself out of it.

Jaxson's eyebrows shot up. "You want her to hang out here, with us?"

"Sure. Maybe I just need to get to know her better. I wasn't in a great place when we met."

He studied her face for a moment, trying to make sure this was what she wanted. She wasn't sure what her face looked like because she had no idea what she wanted. After a moment, he picked up his phone and proceeded to text Lilah.

Cory bit the cuticle on her thumb as she watched. His broad shoulders hunched slightly forward as his thumbs flew over the phone. She liked being able to study him. He was taller than she was and strong. His blue eyes were mesmerizing.

A short bark of laughter pulled her out of her assessment.

He looked up and said to her, "she suggested bowling."

"Bowling?" Cory asked incredulously.

"Yeah, bowling, do you want to? We don't have to."

"I've never actually done it before." She said dubiously.

"Really?"

Cory nodded.

"It's settled then, we have to go bowling." He smiled.

He noted her hesitant expression before adding, "It will be fun. I'll teach you."

She pursed her lips. His smile softened as he reached to stroke the back of her neck. "I know you'll especially love the shoes." He gently kissed her cheek. "Plus, I am an excellent teacher."

He kissed the corner of her mouth.

"Maybe you'll love it so much, you'll want to join a bowling league."

"That could happen." She winked at him.

They grinned at each other before Jaxson returned to his texting.

A short time later, they arrived hand in hand at the bowling alley. He got them shoes and a lane while Cory stared at her surroundings in awe. The bowling alley was loud and dark, punctuated with multiple flashing neon lights.

She gave Jaxson a mischievous smile. "I think I saw this place in a movie from the 80's."

"You love it and you know it." He teased.

"I secretly do." She agreed solemnly.

Their banter was interrupted by Lilah who approached their booth awkwardly.

"Lilah, you made it." Jaxson seemed unfazed. Cory managed a tight smile and tried to steel herself against the ugly comments that were sure to pour from Lilah's mouth.

To her surprise, Lilah smiled and thanked Cory for inviting her. Taken aback, Cory said nothing. The first game was uncomfortable, Cory and Lilah barely interacted while Jaxson carried on a conversation for all three of them.

During the second game, they were able to relax slightly. The atmosphere became almost friendly when Lilah bowled a strike, followed by a strike from Cory, and a gutter ball by Jaxson.

"Beginners luck," Jaxson growled.

"You know you love it." Cory taunted as she confidently strolled into the lane for her next turn. She bowled an unapologetic gutter ball.

"Yeah, I love it and I am extremely jealous of your mad skills." He deadpanned causing Cory to snort before he reached over and gave her a bear hug.

After the third game, Lilah returned her shoes and went to scout out a relatively quiet booth so they could talk.

"I should get us some snacks," Jaxson said, looking toward the food counter.

Cory gave a slight smile and responded, "Jaxson, I already ordered us pizza and drinks. They will be delivered to our table shortly."

So, it was a tiny lie. She did plan on getting snacks. She just hadn't gotten to it yet. Lilah would never know, she assured herself.

"You did?" He asked, "That's awesome. Thank you, Cory." He said while he leaned down for a chaste kiss.

They sat together in the corner booth across from Lilah. Cory was surprised to see an apprehensive look on Lilah's face. She thought they had made significant progress toward at least being friendly with each other. She wondered what made Lilah look so uneasy now.

"Everything okay, Lilah?" Jaxson asked.

Lilah looked dazed for a moment before her eyes settled on Cory. A look of understanding crossed her face.

"Cory, something's going on. I am not sure what it is, but I wonder. Did you, um," she stuttered before speaking again. "Did you say something just a minute ago, something that wasn't true?"

Cory's face froze as her face noticeably blushed, affirming Lilah's question.

Lilah nodded her head as if she were answering her own question. She appeared to gather her thoughts before she spoke again, "I am really glad you invited me here today. I have been trying to figure out a way to talk to you to find out more, but I think I got it."

Cory couldn't hide her surprise, "you've been wanting to talk to me, again? Why?" Her eyes remained locked on Lilah's.

Lilah squirmed in her seat, searching for the words she wanted to say. Jaxson's arm tensed around Cory as if anticipating what Lilah was going to say. Finally, Lilah started, "something has been happening lately. It's been out of the ordinary. I am not sure what it all means, but I know I have to tell you. You have to understand that what you do can have implications and that you have to stop."

Cory arched what would have been an eyebrow if she had one and glanced pointedly at Jaxson. She couldn't believe Lilah would talk about anything family related in front of Jaxson when she was so hung up on keeping secrets.

Lilah shook her head quickly. "No, Cory. Jaxson is fine. He knows everything. He's one of us."

Cory gasped and unconsciously slid further away from Jaxson's hold.

Lilah didn't notice Cory's hesitation as she stared intently at her twined fingers sitting on top of the table. It was Jaxson that leaned in to whisper, "not like that, Cory. We aren't related by blood, but we do share the secret."

Cory glanced at him wanting to discuss it further but stopped when Jaxson minutely shook his head to let her know they would talk about it later. Cory focused her gaze back to Lilah as she felt herself tense as if she were ready to pounce.

She watched closely as Lilah seemed to struggle with what to say. Lilah didn't seem to be acting like herself at all. Cory wasn't sure what to make of it. She unconsciously held her breath and narrowed her eyes, waiting for Lilah to speak.

"It's been happening and I didn't know what it meant. It started after you moved here and I didn't get it, not at first." Lilah said, almost incoherently. "Then just now, I felt it again just a few minutes ago. It felt like a wave or a pulse in the air. Maybe I felt it strongly because you were here with me. I don't know."

Cory and Jaxson shared a look that was part confusion and part concern.

Lilah continued, "You didn't say you did it, but you didn't say you didn't. I think you meant that you told a lie. I think what I felt means that I know when you..." She seemed to be searching for the right words, "when you aren't telling the truth, I can feel it." Her words came out in a rushed whisper.

Cory glowered at Lilah. Jaxson gasped, "the pizza."

They all sat in uncomfortable silence.

Cory sensed that Lilah couldn't take the quiet. It

was something Cory would file away in her mind, Lilah didn't seem to have many weaknesses. It was clear to all three of them that Cory wasn't going to ask for more information. Lilah took a deep breath and started talking. Her words were rushed as she unloaded. "Our family has stories. They have helped guide us over time, but none of them have prepared us for what is happening now. None of our stories describe one of us knowing when another creates truth. I talked with Nonna, um, sorry, your Great-Grandmother about it and we think that maybe, maybe it means something we need to pay attention to."

"So, you know when I lie. You get a feeling when I do it. You don't understand it and you think it means something, right?" Cory clarified.

Lilah shifted uneasily. She had grown up believing the stories and the importance of truth and secrecy. "Cory," she whispered, "We think it means I need to help you speak only the truth. I know the stories of what happened when our family didn't use our gift wisely. We were hunted and killed. Our family was near extinction. We have a powerful gift and it must be protected. I think my role is to help keep our family secret." She glanced at Jaxson, "I am not a physical protector, I think I am more of a secret keeper."

Lilah sat staring at her fingers intertwined on her lap. Cory's gaze stayed on Lilah's face. They sat without moving for several seconds. "I don't get it. Why have a gift if you can't use it?"

"It isn't safe and we must protect ourselves and our family." Lilah leaned across the table to look directly into her eyes. "I was designated the next in line to take care of the family a long time ago. I spent years working with the grandmothers to learn everything I could. I can feel it when you lie. It has to mean something."

Lilah fidgeted in the booth before continuing, "at first I didn't know you were talking, I had trouble figuring it out. It started after you moved here. They were such pulses of heat, almost like a gust of energy. It was different from anything else I have ever experienced. It happened again right before Jaxson told me he was going to the dance with you. I was certain what I felt had something to do with you. I can't explain it. I don't know why. None of our stories have prepared us. I am pretty sure every time you lie, I feel a change in energy. I am like a lie detector for you, Cory." Lilah looked authentically distressed before she continued, "I don't know what it means for sure, but it has to mean something. I feel like we are supposed to do something and we are supposed to be doing it together. The family needs us."

Cory didn't fully believe what Lilah was saying, but there was no denying her earnestness. Lilah truly believed they were supposed to work together on some greater ill-defined plan that would benefit the family line. Cory wanted to run screaming and never stop. Every part of her wanted to reject the idea of being trapped in family destiny. She had been trapped before in a destiny of special schools and group homes. She knew first-hand what it felt like to have no choice and literally to have no voice. She had no desire to be boxed in without a say ever again.

Lilah and Jaxson spoke with quiet intensity about what Lilah's feelings could mean. Cory said nothing. Her mind wandered to her time with her aunt. She thought about Jaxson becoming her boyfriend, Annaliese's appearance at her school, and the unexpected calendar shoot. She had a boyfriend, a best friend, and a modeling job. She should be happy that everything had fallen into place. She had everything she could want, but none of it was real. None of it was because of her but rather this so-called gift. She'd still be an isolated freak show if she hadn't lied about her life. Everything happened because she had some strange witchy gift. Last time she was trapped by her silence, this time she was trapped by a gift she never asked for. She wanted her life to be hers because she created it honestly. She didn't want anything that didn't truly belong to her.

She quickly wiped away a stray tear that dripped down her cheek before either Jaxson or Lilah noticed.

CHAPTER 39

On Monday, Cory sat with Jaxson and Lilah at lunch. It wasn't uncomfortable. Spending time together at the bowling alley had changed things between them, even before Lilah had spilled her guts about being her own personal lie detector. She supposed Jaxson had been right; she hadn't gotten off to a good start with Lilah. She tried to remember if she'd told anyone she and Lilah were friends. It felt possible that their new acceptance of each other could be due to magic. Almost everything else in her life was supernaturally obtained.

As was becoming usual, Cory kept casually scanning the cafeteria for a glimpse of Annaliese, but she never did see her. Cory was starting to worry that something was wrong with her friend. It was like she had dropped off the face of the Earth. Hopefully, it didn't mean that she already had to switch foster homes without saying goodbye, kind of how Cory left Mrs. Grout to live with Miranda.

Cory shuddered, causing Jaxson to put his arm around her shoulders and squeeze her closer to him. She felt a surge of warmth and protection. It made her smile.

The rest of the day passed quickly. After school, Jaxson was waiting by her locker.

"Hey, beautiful." He said.

She wondered if she would ever get used to Jaxson being hers.

"Hey." She answered with a shy smile.

"I have to get to basketball practice. I was hoping I could stop by afterward, but I'm not sure when we'll get finished."

Embellish

"That's alright, stop by whenever. You'll call me if you don't come over, right?" She asked.

"Definitely." He said breathily before leaning in to brush his lips against hers.

Cory walked dreamily home from school. The sun felt good on her face as did the memory of Jaxson's lips against hers.

She unlocked the door and called out for Miranda.

There was no answer. The house was completely still. Cory was thrilled to realize she was alone.

She walked in to the kitchen and was ecstatic to see a plastic bag with the name of her favorite art store printed on it sitting on the kitchen table. The afternoon was turning into her own version of perfection. In the bag, there was an extra-large drawing pad, watercolor paper, charcoals, oil pastels, and some new tubes of acrylic paint.

She was touched her aunt would think to buy them for her and thrilled to have the new supplies.

She practically skipped to her room where she threw her backpack down unceremoniously in the corner and the bag of supplies reverently on her unmade bed. She pulled off her jewelry and outer layers of clothes until she was left barefoot wearing a black ribbed tank top and a pair of black leggings. She twisted her hair into a bun on top of her head, then turned on some music from her iPod.

She was set to lose herself in art.

She took a sheet of the drawing paper and clipped it onto her easel. She studied it for a moment, thinking about what she wanted to paint. Then she opened one of her dresser drawers and pulled out a bag of brushes and a palette. Then she opened her new tube of white paint. She was going to work in grayscale.

The doorbell rang.

She ignored it. It was too early for Jaxson and she

didn't want to give up a second of her precious time to see who else it could be.

She began to squirt blobs of paint onto her white plastic palette. Next, she'd add a single blob of black to the palette. She'd use it to create her greys. She would need much more white than black to create all the shades she'd want to use.

A frown marred her features as the doorbell rang again.

Cory turned up her iPod. She needed to paint and there was no one she wanted to see.

She picked up her pencil and rotated her shoulders, hoping to loosen them so she could freely sketch the outline for her painting. She felt like she needed a new self-portrait. She wanted to show her inner strength. She studied her face in the mirror and then brought her hand to the paper. She lightly sketched the shape of her face and neck. It was enough to guide her, but not enough to show through the paint that would be eventually applied.

The doorbell rang a third time, followed by pounding. Whoever was there was insistent. Why couldn't they get the hint and go away? She was alone and ready to paint. She didn't want to be interrupted.

Then she heard yelling at the door, a female voice. She couldn't tell who it belonged to. It was clear they weren't going to go away until she answered the door and told them in no uncertain terms that they were not wanted.

"Fine," Cory grumbled. She speared the pencil into her hair at the base of her bun before stalking down the stairs to open the door. The voice got louder, calling her name, as she approached.

Cory was surprised to see a disheveled Annaliese on her front porch.

"Annaliese, hi. What's going on?" Cory asked. Her

annoyance at being interrupted completely melting away.

"Cory, I wanted to talk to you about something. It is really important." She practically shoved Cory aside as she rushed into the room, pulling the door closed behind her.

Feeding on Annaliese's alarm, Cory responded, "Come in. What is it? What's the matter? Why haven't you been in school?"

Annaliese's expression morphed from tension to hatred. Cory took a half a step back to give herself a sense of distance. She couldn't understand the expression on her friend's face. Annaliese gazed icily before she appeared to force herself to speak. "I know about you, Cory. I know what you can do. I know what you did."

Cory felt her eyes widen as she tried to piece together what Annaliese was saying. She was shocked speechless.

"Don't stand there playing dumb with me, Cory." Her voice had lost all traces of being timid. "I know what you can do. You have the gift of creation. You make things from nothing. I've suspected it since we were at the Grouts. You proved it when I got here."

"Annaliese, I have no idea what you are talking about." She really didn't. The ability for lies to come true was one thing, but creation?

Annaliese shut the door behind her and laughed. "You proved it all, Cory. You didn't have to tell me your secret to confirm it."

Cory felt herself go pale. Annaliese knew about her secret. The secret she hadn't told anyone. She wanted to pretend that she didn't understand, but she knew she couldn't. She had been discovered. The only real shock was that it was Annaliese who outted her. But maybe, she reasoned, it would be a relief to be able to talk about it.

"I never meant to. I didn't know anything back then. I never meant to kill Mrs. Grout, even though I didn't touch her. I had no idea, no idea that my words..." Her voice fell away as the tears threatened to spill from her eyes.

Annaliese threw back her head and let out a dark, merciless laugh. "What? You think that was you? You, the weakest, most damaged among them? You think you have that much power?" She snarled at Cory, her face filled with disdain.

"No, it wasn't you. That was all me and you know what, Cory, it was a pleasure." Annaliese's expression twisted with pride. "It didn't take much," Annaliese continued. "She was dying anyway. I just made it happen a little sooner than it would have happened naturally. I barely had to hold the pillow over her face before she was gone."

Cory's blood ran cold while Annaliese's eyes glinted with satisfied fury. "I knew after seeing your eyes that you were from the family I was looking for. You were a little too good at art. I thought you were from the creator's line, but then you didn't talk, so I couldn't be sure if you were the one I needed. When you left, I knew I had to follow. I searched until I found out where you went. Then I got rid of the old lady, moved closer to you, and became your best friend. Someone you could confide in, someone to trust.

"You told me what I needed to know at the coffee shop. Do you remember what you said?"

Cory shook her head, not trusting her voice to speak.

"You told me that I had found a good place, that I was going to be happy, and that I would find my way."

This time Cory took a full step backward, away from Annaliese.

"Don't you remember, Cory?" Annaliese said sweetly. " You said those things to me and of course they have all been coming true. I have found a good place. I am unbelievably happy and I have found my way. I am here to take on your powers."

Cory was dumbfounded.

"Oh yes, Cory, my family has a gift as well, a much better one than yours. We can take on the powers of others. You are limited to your own gift where we can take on the gifts of many."

Cory couldn't believe what she was hearing. Her head spun with dizziness. "But, why?" was all she could manage.

"Because, once I have your powers, I will be able to get more from others. You are not strong, but you are enough. My kind has a secret too, my kind was put on this Earth to find and control yours and all others that have special talents. We aren't governed by rules the way your family is." She spat the words. "Our job is to seek, take, and control."

"That's what happened before wasn't it?" Cory asked, suddenly filled with understanding. "Your family was responsible for taking our powers and killing us off."

Annaliese's lips turned up in a sinister smile that didn't reach her eyes. "Maybe you're not as dumb as you look. But you know what, nobody will ever know. I am going to take your powers and send you to shadows."

Before Cory could respond, a blur moved from behind her and pounced directly on Annaliese.

Cory screamed in horror. Annaliese was fighting with someone. It was snarling chaos. She backed up, trying ineffectively to escape. The fight in front of her was inhumanly fast. Her eyes searched for anything she could use as a weapon. She had to be able to defend herself when they turned their attention to her.

Before she could take a step, a shimmering light blinded her before the room became deathly quiet.

Cory's eyes darted back to the fight. She was surprised to see Jaxson pushing himself up from the floor. Annaliese was nowhere to be seen.

He looked Cory in the eye and said, "Her kind was made to find and control, but she forgot. My kind was made to keep you protected."

Cory's mouth hung open in shock. Her brain was trying to make sense of everything Annaliese had said, Jaxson's sudden presence, the fight, and Annaliese's unexplained disappearance. It was too much. Her head swam sickeningly before a curtain of blackness closed in around her.

CHAPTER 40

Cory recognized the voices before she opened her eyes. She heard Jaxson, Lilah, and another voice. It took her a moment to realize the voice belonged to her neighbor. Why was Mr. Bradley here?

"They know she's here and they know she has a gift. We have to do something. We need to run. We need to go deeper into hiding. We must start over. They will be after all of us." Lilah urged.

"We need to talk with your grandmothers, Lilah. We don't know how she found us, and besides, Jaxson defeated her. Everyone will be safe for now. I can work with him, help him become even stronger." Mr. Bradley said.

Cory was confused, wondering what they could possibly be talking about. Her head swam with Annaliese's words. Annaliese called her a creator. Her art had tipped her off. Her gift wasn't just words that became true. Her gift was in creating. Her art was a part of the gift.

Cory felt sick. Her art was the one thing she could count on. It was the one thing she thought was truly hers. She thought it was what made her special.

"We can do this, Lilah. I can feel it. I can keep her safe." Jaxson added. His words distracted Cory from her thoughts.

"It isn't just her, Jaxson. It's all of us. Can you keep us all safe?" Lilah snapped.

Cory's mind spun. Were they talking about keeping her safe? Where did Annaliese go? Would she be back? Then a fuzzy memory came back to her. It was something Lilah had said at the bowling alley, something about her being a secret keeper and Jaxson being a protector.

Something clicked in place in her mind. If Jaxson

was a protector and he came to save her when Annaliese was about to siphon away her gift, then he must be a protector for her. He was here to protect the family gift. He wasn't hers. She was nothing more than an object in need of protection.

She felt her pulse thudding in her ears.

He wasn't spending time with her because he cared about her. He cared about the family gift. He wasn't really her boyfriend. It was an illusion. Her art wasn't even hers. It was a trick of the gift. How could she have been so stupid?

She started to feel suffocated like she couldn't get a breath. None of it was real. It was just another form of control. She didn't have a boyfriend who liked her for her. She wasn't talented. She wasn't even an artist. Not really. She made things happen because she was a freak with teal eyes and a supernatural gift. She wasn't special.

She needed to be in control. She had to make her own decisions and live with the outcomes. It was the only way her life could be hers. She had to live on her own terms. Independence. It was the one thing she needed and she would never be able to have it if she lived with her family legacy.

She feigned unconsciousness as she hashed out a plan. She had to break free.

After what felt like a long time, she was ready. For better or worse, she would be on her own and that was something she could live with. She slowly opened her eyes and cleared her throat alerting the others that she was awake.

"Cory." Jaxson breathed before rushing to her side and grasping her hand. She wished she could melt into it and accept Jaxson as her boyfriend, but she couldn't.

Not now that she knew the truth. She couldn't continue to live a false life. She had to be the one in charge of what happened to her.

"You're a protector." She said in a matter of fact tone.

"Yes." He acknowledged.

"Your job is to protect the gift."

"The gift yes, but most importantly, my job is to protect you." He said.

"Why?"

"It's always been that way. When the gift was given, a protector was assigned. As the gift was passed along through descendants, so was the role of the protector." Mr. Bradley answered.

"Lilah?" Cory asked, "Who is your protector?"

Lilah looked down at her clasped hands and whispered. "I'm not sure. I always thought it was Jaxson, but when you came, things changed." Her voice trailed off.

Lilah said nothing for a moment, before thoughtfully continuing, "I realized he was never my protector. He was supposed to be yours. I seem to be something different. I told you, I seem to be the secret keeper. Maybe I am supposed to be your guide of sorts because I feel when you use your gift. I don't really know why."

Cory felt sorry for Lilah. She had seemed so confident and authoritative when they met. She knew all about the family history and the gift. It was shocking to see her so uncertain.

"Mr. Bradley, what about you?" Cory asked.

"I have also been a protector. I have aided the grandmothers and now I help watch family members who do not seem to have the gift but who have teal colored eyes. If they end up showing signs of having the gift my job was to let the grandmothers, now Lilah, know so they can make sure the secret is kept."

His words were soft and kind, his personality was like an indulgent grandfather, but they struck Cory in exactly the wrong way. His words solidified her resolve to go along with her plan. Everything about the family was about being hidden and controlled. It wasn't about living. She had to live her life on her own terms. She wasn't going to hide unspeaking at her old school and she wasn't going to hide in the family under the guard of a protector who posed as her boyfriend. She was finished. She had to break free. She was going to find herself, her true self. She wasn't an artist, that was the gift. She needed the real her.

She would tell one more lie to get away.

Or maybe a set of lies.

She wouldn't even consider them to be lies. She would simply alter the facts. She would embellish the truth and then she would never use her gift again. She would break free of the gift and from all of them, once and for all.

She looked Lilah in the eye and spoke clearly so there would be no misunderstanding. She had to be strong and choose her words carefully. "Lilah, there are no family stories about what you feel, because you feel nothing when I lie. Jaxson," she shifted her gaze to meet Jaxson's, "I broke up with you because I got an offer to attend an exclusive school for the arts because of a contest, Mr. Smythe my art teacher, entered me in. They didn't want me for my art. I don't do art anymore. They wanted me as a model."

All three gaped at her, obviously trying to make sense of what she was saying.

She glanced at their faces. Reassured she was doing the right thing, she continued, "Miranda is excited for me and has allowed me to go. I will be moving there by the end of the week. Nobody will come after me, I will forget all about the gift and about all of you. I am not a part of any family stories because I do not have a gift. I never did. I will never tell the family secret because I will only speak the truth from now on."

A small, sad smile curved Cory's lips. She was losing so much but she didn't have a choice. She would not live a life governed by rules over a gift she didn't want. She would make her own destiny by denying the one she was born with.

She heard Jaxson whisper an anguished, "no."

"Cory, no. It is more than that. You can't walk away. We have to work together." Lilah cried.

Cory was briefly surprised that her words didn't instantly seem to become true. She wasn't supposed to be a part of any of it anymore. She pushed the thought out of her mind. She couldn't worry about it. She had to keep working her plan.

"I need you all to leave. I have to pack." She calmly stood and slowly walked to her room knowing they all sat in stunned silence.

Without looking back, she closed and locked the door to her room behind her. She turned up her iPod and tried to ignore the itch in her hands to pick up a pencil or brush. Her natural reaction was to paint or draw. She wanted more than anything to lose herself in her art but she wouldn't.

Never again.

After brushing tears from her cheeks, she pulled a box out of her closet and began hurrying to fill it with her art supplies. She needed them gone before she was tempted to use them.

To be continued.

= = =

MEET THE AUTHOR

Kelley Connor has helped hundreds of babies be born in her role as a labor and delivery nurse. She has degrees in nursing and studio art. She started writing stories with her children as a creative outlet and to help them become better readers. Her children would give her an idea, she would write a story about it, then they would read it together. Her daughters are her biggest cheerleaders and her harshest critics. Kelley enjoys reading and writing about the supernatural, technology, and science fiction. In her spare time, she enjoys planning and taking travel adventures, gardening, and exploring the Idaho outdoors with her husband, kids, and giant, yellow, mutt of a dog, Jax.

ACKNOWLEDGEMENTS

Thank you to Stephanie Krischuk who has been my sounding board, partner in crime, and friend for more years than I can count.

- Kelley Connor